Of the Wing

The Ivory-billed Obsession

Georgia Anne Butler

PINCHEY HOUSE PRESS
KYLERTOWN, PENNSYLVANIA

Printed in the United States of America

This is a work of fiction. Characters portrayed do not represent living or deceased individuals (except for Sammy, the sheepdog).

ISBN-13: 978-0-9820342-2-4
Library of Congress Control Number: 2011906219

CPSIA Tracking: 072011-1-1000-JO-16803

Cover Design and title page illustration by Karl Eric Leitzel

For Kathy

Acknowledgments

Foremost, I acknowledge Kathleen M. O'Dell, my sister, who in one sentence provided me the causal agent for this story's plot. In life, generally, Kathy is always prepared to provide me with whatever I need—emotional support, inspiration, friendship, or love.

I want to also acknowledge and thank Allan J. Mueller for his hospitality and expertise. Allan generously extended to me an invitation to join him and his close friends on a two-day canoe trip of Bayou DeView (Arkansas), the site of several sightings in past years of the Ivory-billed Woodpecker. This adventure and access to Allan's knowledge of the Ivory-bill's habitat and habits made it possible for me to write *The Ivory-billed Obsession.*

In April 2009, Matt Conner, then a park ranger with the White River National Wildlife Refuge, gave me a motorboat tour of Moon Lake and Indian Bayou and thereafter drove me to several locations of interest. His suggestion that I visit the Champion Tree was one I followed to my great benefit. Thus I write here to thank Matt for his time, information, and advice.

Others who assisted me in various ways include Christina Verderosa, Dan Scheiman, Pat and Eddie Lumsden, and David Luneau. Thank you all.

Author's Note

My story includes two Native American characters, father and son, of the Pueblo people of Cochiti. The Cochiti of New Mexico speak a dialect of an oral language called Keres. Today, members of the Cochiti pueblo are in disagreement as to whether their language should be preserved as an oral tradition or translated into a spelling system for preservation and teaching. Within this story I have chosen to include a few words from their own orthography (spelling system).

I also chose to use a fictional surname for the story's Cochiti characters to assure no unintended association to real people.

Contents

Of the Wing
The Ivory-billed Obsession

1

Rattlesnake Trail

The timber rattlesnake glided over the outcrop, intent on satisfying a growing hunger. Morning sun glistened on the burnt orange stripe tracking a line down his stout body. His triangular head sought a large crevice on the outcrop's edge, giving access to the rock face below. Deep into the crack the snake fed his winding body, moving ever downward, until at last even his thorny rattle disappeared. As the fissure narrowed, the snake pushed outward to the rock face, following a slim ledge plunging downward.

He knew the way.

For some years the snake had hunted this woodland territory, leaving when the small rodents declined in number and returning when they rose. The mice, chipmunks, and rats on which he fed were also foods of his competitors, the hawks and owls. And too often these opponents sought the same warm morsel. How many times had the patient rattler waited, coiled by some path, only to lose his meal to a greedy hawk or owl?

Down he slid to where the rock lip tapered into the cliff side, directly above an alcove holding a hawk nest. With broad head dipping into the open space of the recess, the snake sensed heat. And as this heat pulled him nearer, the vertical

Chapter 1

pupils of his eyes fastened onto the downy white fluff of big-eyed hatchlings.

Claire had not noticed the snake descending toward the nest, a huge cradle of sticks lined with soft strips of bark. It lay tucked within a deep ledge, fifteen feet from the surface of the rock formation known as the Finger. From her position on the neighboring outcrop, the Fist, she might easily have seen him through her binoculars but for watching elsewhere. The subject of her study was the female Red-tailed Hawk that she and her friend Victor called Ku-Khain, a Cochiti word for the color red. Her friend Victor, half Pueblo Indian, had given the hawk this beautiful, secret name. Locals called the enormous raptor Big Red.

Not allowed to go alone to the outcrop, Claire went anyway. And if asked simply omitted reference to time spent there. After all, she was almost 12 and certainly old enough to take care of herself. Besides, who else would daily accompany her to this isolated spot in the woods? No one—because no one cared for Ku-Khain as much as she.

Ku-Khain had flown from her mothering tasks at the cliff side nest in response to her mate's call. He had a tender young gray squirrel, freshly killed, to give her. A much smaller hawk, the male awaited his female on the highest horizontal branch of a dying oak. This oak, rooted in a nearby precipice, was a favorite perching site for the pair because it provided an expansive view for hunting and quick access to their nest.

After the food transfer, while she ate, he would return to the hatchlings.

As Ku-Khain grabbed the squirrel from her mate, the timber rattler wound his thick, long body around the unattended nest. And as Claire breathlessly watched the female eviscerate the squirrel, the snake dislocated his jaw to accommodate one of her three downy chicks.

His mate hungrily eating, the male hawk (named Hakanyi for "fire") launched into the sky to head back to the nest. Claire paid him no mind, too absorbed in the blood feast of Ku-Khain, until—

Tsee eee arrr!!!

A scream of defiance pierced the air.

Spotting the predator, Hakanyi dove with folded wings toward the nest, rearing up and back to grab the intruder as the snake struck toward the pulse of his pounding wings. Both talon and fang missed their marks.

Ku-Khain dropped her squirrel and launched into battle flight as Claire fumbled the binoculars down the bridge of her nose. Pulling these again to her eyes, she rushed forward to follow the hawk's trajectory, unaware of her position so near the cliff edge. A couple strides more and her foot would drop through the air. She took a lunging step with her right foot just as her left ankle gave out and so stumbled forward. With outstretched arms she sought to break the fall, but her bracing limbs plunged beyond the cliff's edge. She saw the ground 30

Chapter 1

feet below within the frame of her extended arms and thought, "I'm going to die."

Her chest slammed against the rock's surface, knocking all breath from her lungs. For some seconds she lay, stunned, her head, shoulders and arms hanging limp over the cliff side. Insensitive to the world about her, Claire did not then witness the life and death struggle between the hawks and the snake. Neither did the female hawk note the draping form of an adolescent girl, past whom she had sped an instant before combat.

Flapping heavily to gain altitude for a second strike, Hakanyi lost his opportunity to Ku-Khain, who swooped past with a searing scream and a gush of air. Like the male, she reared back, extending her talons as the rattler sprang toward a muscular leg, fangs targeting flesh. Ku-Khain caught the streaking flash in a crushing claw and, pulling back, drew the snake's entire length free of the rock shelf. Instantly, the hawk sank downward, as an anchor in the sea. Clutched only by the head, the snake thrashed his stout, long body in the open air. Ku-Khain tried to gain altitude but continued to sink with the weight of her cargo until the male dove beneath to seize the snake by its mid-section. With burden distributed, the two headed upward and toward their oak perch to finish the killing job.

Flying with the snake strung between, the two hawks reached an altitude equal to that of Claire's prostrate body and passed only feet from her uplifting head. What passed before

4

her unfocused eyes appeared absurd: two huge prehistoric birds carrying a glistening bronze garland through a beautiful blue sky. The dazed girl closed her eyes and opened them to look again, only to see the more distant birds wrestling this same garland, one end of which was dropped. An instant later, the garland was toppling earthward.

Claire's head dropped and for several more moments she lay draped like something dead over the cliff's edge. When again she roused, her body felt pain and her mind tried to decipher the reason. She looked downward to the distant ground and its scrubby vegetation and then noted the arms hanging by her head like a Raggedy Ann doll. She raised her head but not the heavy arms rooting her to the rock face.

Now she felt her lungs struggling to fill fully with air and her rib cage pressing against an immovable surface. She felt the binocular strap cutting across her cheek. With each recognized sensation, her mind supplied a fragment of memory until an image of what happened filled her mind. She panicked. Adrenalin surged through her body. Hoisting her head and shoulders, she braced elbows against the cliff edge. Using more will than strength, she inched herself backward, wiggling side to side, until clear of the overhang.

While the girl lay recovering on the rock face, the mated hawks had returned to the hatchlings. The male hopped on to the nest's edge to deliver a morsel of raw meat as Ku-Khain, now perched atop the outcrop, watched the snow-headed human squirming atop the neighboring rock.

Chapter 1

The female hawk did not fear or distrust the snow-headed one, though her new mate did. Daily he dove at the girl, screaming defiance at her presence on the neighboring outcrop. But with each attack, the human intruder simply ducked to the ground, covering herself with a dense yet removable hide. Such scenes played out again and again until finally he tired of the repetition and chose instead to watch her with steely eyes.

Aching and scared, Claire finally rose to her knees and then to her feet, walking unsteadily off the outcrop. In the slow march through the woods toward home she had much to occupy her mind. In the distance, a fast-plodding black and white shaggy hulk moved through a green world. So precisely timed were her dog's arrivals, Claire wondered if the sheepdog couldn't somehow read her mind. For they had reached an agreement: to arrive and leave together but otherwise go their separate ways. And no matter how long she stayed at the outcrop, somehow Sammy always returned in time to intercept her path on the way out.

With Sammy again Claire felt better, though stiff, and began to attend to the sounds of singing birds. The high choir of dawn had ended hours since, yet many songsters whistled or trilled their tunes from the canopies of newly leaved trees.

Claire was an avid birder but even more—she kept birds in her heart. And with its every beat, her heart broadcast a love so strong that birds were drawn to it. At least that's how she understood it. So Claire wasn't surprised to hear the buzzy whistling phrases of a Scarlet Tanager, especially since a pair of these birds adorned her chartreuse sweatshirt. Whether mere coincidence or something more . . . whatever bird Claire wore on her clothing was certain to appear to her that same day in flesh or in song.

Turning homeward, she withdrew into the fortress of her mind, walking without seeing or hearing, focused entirely on her thoughts. Even Jerry wouldn't approve of her solitary trips to the outcrop—especially if he knew that she used his heavy hooded coat as protection against the male hawk's dive-bombing attacks. And if anyone should be sympathetic to her case, it was Jerry. He was the scruffy old man she met six months earlier, in this same woodland. When she met him, the leaves were colorful but dying; now they were fresh from the tight buds of spring. No less spectacular had been Jerry's transformation in her life: from a rumored lunatic known by locals as the "Chicken Man" to an adopted family member. Even her mother had taken to him so quickly that now Jerry boarded in their home—with his pet chicken Becky and homing pigeon Patty—helping with the family business, a one-room country grocery.

Something in the distance passed through her peripheral vision. Instinct told her to drop from view, but Sammy charged toward the intruder, freezing him in his steps. With no choice, she trotted after the sheepdog.

"He won't bite," she yelled, voice carrying the distance. Then recognizing the figure, she faltered. Only a hundred feet separated her from Billy, until recently her constant enemy. Dealing with the 14-year-old had become confusing since forming a truce with him, one thrust upon them by Victor. Two weeks earlier, while visiting the outcrop with her, Victor had been attacked by Hakanyi. Stuck high up a tree, Claire couldn't help her only friend crouching helplessly beneath the hawk's diving assaults. Then, miraculously, Billy had darted onto the outcrop, pulling Victor to safety.

Billy didn't explain how he came to be there and Victor didn't ask. He only insisted that she and Billy put an end to their animosity. And for a few short hours, they did. Claire forgot her resentment of the school bully who regularly taunted her, and Billy forgot his extreme jealousy of the strangely pale girl with the boyishly short, white hair who sought to take his place in Victor's life.

But their truce couldn't last.

Sammy jumped up at the tall, wiry teen, greeting him like a long-lost friend. Billy wore baggy, ripped cut-offs and a faded black tee shirt, crudely altered with a pair of scissors to be sleeveless.

"Get your dog off me," he said, in his typically surly way.

"Rub his head a bit," she countered. "That's all he wants."

Billy dropped a hand awkwardly onto Sammy's head and then yanked it away.

"That's enough, Sammy," Claire said, pulling the huge sheepdog by the collar as the boy moved beyond reach of his straining paws. "What'cha doing?" She snatched a glance at his long, big-featured face before looking away. As always, Billy concealed his glass eye behind a pad of oily brown hair, which he consistently stroked to keep in place.

"What business of it is yours?" he said, lip curling beneath a long nose.

"Be that way!" Claire turned abruptly but Sammy again bounded toward the boy. And again she wrestled to pull him away. "I hope you're not heading to the outcrop," she said, no longer avoiding his face. "Because that male hawk *will* attack you." In truth, she wasn't concerned about what Hakanyi might do to him but what he might do to the hawks. A known delinquent, Billy had once tried and failed to shoot Ku-Khain. Moreover, his father, a fugitive from law, had obsessively stalked the legendary raptor intending to stuff her as a trophy.

Claire noted a full backpack slung over one of his shoulders. At least he wasn't toting a rifle or shotgun. "What do you have in that backpack?"

Already turning away, Billy glanced back. "Wouldn't you like to know?"

"I know what you're up to," she said defiantly, having not the least idea. But when Billy reacted with open-mouthed astonishment, she trumpeted, "I knew it! You ARE up to no good." Oafish features contracting in relief, he said, "You don't know squat," and turned to stomp through the underbrush, following no particular trail. Straining to hold Sammy back, Claire watched the boy recede into the woods, heading who knows where.

2

A Billion-Dollar Idea

Though Claire intended to head directly home, Sammy had different intentions. He bounded up a low, boulder-studded crest, alerting the canine radar of one standard but very strong beagle—Moon Doggy. Through a host of young white birch trees off in the distance sat a barn and beside it a doghouse. At the end of a chain, the beagle howled as the sheepdog rushed toward him. Claire hurried now so as not to irritate the property owner, a high-strung widow, not of typical mentality.

Moon Doggy was waiting, pacing at the end of his chain. Here he remained forgotten by the widow all the day long but for a daily meal and watering. Such wasn't the case, even a year ago, when the widow's husband was alive. Mike had been inseparable from the beagle, spending many long hours hunting with him in the woods. And if Mike wasn't hunting, he was with Jerry (and Becky, the Rhode Island Red, who appeared as an appendage growing from Jerry's broad shoulders). Together all four would visit the outcrop to spend long afternoons.

Her husband's constant absence made Helen Whiner mad. She resented the beagle; even more, she resented Jerry. So when her husband died suddenly, and Jerry came to adopt the dog, she refused him out of spite. And out of spite the poor, hapless dog spent his days lonely and bored—but not this moment.

This moment the beagle spun in excitement, thrilled by the visit of the girl. Weeks before this girl had taken him from the chain to run through the woods under the full moon and to swim in the creek and to chase the porcupines into trees. Maybe she would take him from the chain now, maybe, maybe, maybe . . .

He spun in delirious circles.

But Claire couldn't stay. She lavished him with praise and stroked his belly while he peddled the air, running as fast as he might. Sammy sniffed the floppy ears that lay upright alongside the beagle's head, giving him a sweet, comical look.

"Don't worry, Moon Doggy. I'll come back for you soon," she said, rising to leave, "even if you do smell like dirty socks."

The beagle's real name, the one given him as a puppy a dozen years earlier, was Schooner. But Jerry nicknamed him Moon Doggy, because once a month, on the full moon, he'd walked the beagle at midnight. Without Helen Whiner's permission or even her knowledge, the man and dog would roam the woods all night long.

Not wishing to be caught by the irritable woman, Claire stealthily crept past the barn, situated below the house at the bottom of a wooded hillside. Remarkably, Moon Doggy did not bark after them but stood squarely, ears pricked, watching as they faded back into the woods.

Chapter 2

Within the soothing green cover of trees again, Sammy bounding ahead, Claire felt relieved to have escaped detection. The widow was a bizarre woman, cranky and yet somehow childlike in her ferocious attachment to things and ideas. Once Helen had nearly pushed her off the side porch, demanding that she chase Billy, her grand nephew. He had fled from the kitchen as she charged, ready to pull and bobby pin the hair from off his glass eye. (Helen was obsessed with pinning her own straggly, gray hair in tight coils to her scalp with bobby pins.) That day Billy had called his great Aunt Helen "crazy," but Claire knew them all to be troubled. At least Helen was likeable in an odd-bird sort of way. The same could not be said of Billy, and especially not of his father, Clyde Hollow. Billy's father, a jobless drunkard who lived in a rusting, abandoned school bus, took odd jobs for cash, including cleaning his Aunt Helen's pigeon loft. That's how Claire had first encountered him. Even now just thinking of Clyde Hollow made her shudder.

That evening, Claire's mother Louise pulled two aluminum lounge chairs out into the open field above the large pond, ringed by bullfrogs preparing for the evening's chorus. Only May, the air yet held a springtime chill. She looked far across the property to the warm light of her daughter's upstairs bedroom. There, Claire was removing the blue-tinted contacts worn to conceal her golden eyes. Louise reclined on the lounge, wrapped in a blanket and the sounds and smells of

12

approaching summer. At six feet, she stood taller than most men. With broad, straight shoulders, she was a woman of formidable stature and pleasant disposition. She loved nothing or no one more than Claire.

Without the blessing of a daughter, the young woman would have fared much worse after losing her husband to a trucking accident. At the time Claire was just old enough to comfort her mother the way only little ones know how. "Don't be sad, mommy," she'd say, golden eyes huge with sincerity. "You can sleep with me tonight, and I'll let you hold the pink pony." And many a night Louise did cling to the little girl with long, gentle curls covering her narrow shoulders like snow. But when time came to send her to kindergarten, Louise couldn't let go. And so she home schooled Claire, both in the certified curriculum and all that was meaningful to herself and the child's father—the natural world.

Hopping across the cold, wet grass in bare feet, Claire joined her mother.

"Claire, go put shoes on!"

But the stubborn adolescent sank quickly into the chaise, wrapping her feet, stinging of cold, within the woolen blanket draped there. "I'm already tucked in, mother," she said, flashing a winning grin. Overhead little brown bats swept the air with fast beating wings in search of insects. Around the field they flew, crisscrossing the sky and diving after moth and mosquito.

Chapter 2

Each evening, after the store closed, mother and daughter spent time together comparing their days. With so much change in their lives, both had plenty to report. Claire was completing the sixth grade but her first year in public school. And Louise was finally living her dream as an entrepreneur and owner of a small country store—a long, large room fronting half an historic wood frame house, over 150 years old. Though situated in a hollow, along a creek, the house sat above the floodplain on a modest swell of ground, protected from west winds and weather by a hillside of wild cherry trees that led up to an expansive pasture. To the north and south lay more pasture while an extensive woodland, many hundreds of acres large, lay to their east, bordering the property.

Jerry sometimes joined the pair but always later, giving them ample time to talk. He boarded with them, paying for his food and room by working in the store. By most standards his accommodations would appear meager—a narrow upstairs storage space converted to a bedroom—but to Jerry it was perfect. More perfect still in that his room's high transom window, when fitted with a small exterior shelf, suited well as a landing area and trap for his homing pigeon. Thus part of his room, one-third at least, was devoted to his birds, their accommodations behind a chicken-wire wall, which he kept scrupulously clean.

This evening Louise updated Claire on her favorite topic, one daily discussed by her regular customers: the pending visit of a certain celebrity. Robert Crawley was an ornithologist who traveled the world on birding expeditions. His "Life List" of birds identified was the largest of any birder in the world, or so he claimed. In a few days Crawley was headed to Pennsylvania to inhabit the woodland chateau that otherwise stood unoccupied for months, even years. The retreat, watched over by an old caretaker, sat on a high point above the West Branch of the Susquehanna, at the end of a climbing, winding private road. A locked iron gate at the bottom barred curious sightseers.

For weeks, news of the eccentric billionaire's coming visit had been reported in the local newspaper, accompanied by photos taken from prior visits. And in these photos Claire first saw the smiling, handsome man standing before his extravagant limestone chateau. The building, described by locals as a fortress, was an extravagant stone structure with turrets, like those seen in European castles, but on a much smaller scale.

"I didn't realize how nearby Mr. Crawley's chateau is," Louise said, lowering the chair back to better see the first stars blinking into existence. "Maybe he'll come into the store."

"Do you think so?" The preteen sprang upright. Her interest in the man was acute. He represented everything she longed to be and do—an ornithologist traveling the world to see and study birds. And he was incredibly attractive.

"Possibly," Louise said, smiling. She could see that her daughter had a crush.

Claire lay back into the chair, tucking the wool blanket under her thighs and pulling it up over her arms. "I feel so badly for him. He's been searching for that Ivory-billed Woodpecker for years, ever since those men caught it on video."

"That's what I read," Louise said. "Everyone thought the woodpecker was extinct."

"And he was in Arkansas again just two months ago and still didn't find it." Louise rocked her head in mock sympathy for the unfortunate billionaire. "I bet I could find that woodpecker," Claire said, with a decided nod.

Absorbed in the stars bulging from the deepening darkness, Louise forgot to agree and instead pointed to a bright white star just above. "Look. The brightest stars are just beginning to shine."

In a fresh day filled with sunshine and birdsong, Jerry and Claire worked together in the vegetable garden. Jerry cut heads of lettuce as Claire pulled spring onions from the earth. "I love the smell of dirt," she said, plucking another plump onion from the ground over which she crouched.

Jerry stood with a slight grunt from his bent position, a head of romaine clutched in his hand. "It's soil." He threw the lettuce into a wheelbarrow with a half dozen other heads. "Dirt is what you sweep from the kitchen floor."

"Yeah, that's right," she said, smirking up at the aged man whose mission this morning seemed to be her enlightenment.

Yet that was okay since it also meant she could more easily coax information from him on another topic—the location of Robert Crawley's lodge. She had asked earlier at the breakfast table, pretending a vague curiosity. And so he had answered vaguely, never suspecting her intention to plan a scouting expedition there with Victor. She studied Jerry, pondering how to yet again raise the topic without raising his suspicions.

Jerry seemed both old and young to her. Though his hair had grayed, it hadn't thinned, a quality her mother commented on every time she cut it. And the face above his long, trimmed beard was taut, not loose or fleshy like many older people. But most youthful were his eyes: a blue-green blend that absorbed the light of either color. So sometimes his eyes could appear green as a summer pond or blue as a late afternoon sky.

Claire dug at the soil around another onion. "Jerry," she said, not looking upward but noting the swing of his head in her direction. "I was just wondering—"

Through a row of radishes ran Becky, the Rhode Island Red, squawking for attention.

"Don't you ever stop complaining?" Jerry said to his pet chicken, winking at Claire. He squatted to offer his shoulder as a roost, and she obligingly sprung to the thick suede patch he wore to protect himself from her grasping claws. "Let's head up to the pasture."

Claire jumped up, dropping an onion into a basket. "I bet we see Bobolinks up there," she said and ran toward the hillside populated by wild cherry trees.

17

Chapter 2

Jerry ambled behind, shouting after. "That's a safe bet since they've been up there weeks already." On short, stout legs, the man slowly took the incline through the thick grove of young trees while Claire dashed to the top. Halfway up, Becky fluttered to the ground, scampering back toward the garden that lay at the hill's base. All winter long, Jerry and Louise had planned the large plot to provide lots of fresh produce for the store. He still marveled at the blessing of having found this beautiful family, of which he now was an honorary member.

Jerry found Claire at the top scanning the ground for Bobolinks, a meadow bird whose song was a contraption of whistles, brassy slides, jangles, bells, and chatter—cheerful music that seemed to percolate up through the grass itself.

Sensing his approach, a pair of binoculars bolted to her eyes, Claire snorted in frustration. "They're hidden in the grass and not one will show himself."

Jerry tapped her on the shoulder. "Well sometimes, Claire, you have to look out at the world to see it." And as she lowered the binoculars, he pointed to a male Bobolink, perched atop a bull thistle, just 30 feet away. Keeping utterly still, they watched the black bird with white on his wings and rump. But most conspicuously, the back of his head—from crown to nape—was the color of straw. Whatever magic held the bird poised for their inspection finally vanished as he flew over the growing grasses and then disappeared within.

Turning to walk the path running parallel to the hilltop, Claire again attempted to gain the information she needed. "If Crawley's lodge is five miles as the crow flies, how many miles is it if you were to walk?"

Jerry's open expression contracted. Bushy brows lowering over squinting eyes, he said, "Don't even think about it, little girl." Into her eyes shielded by blue-tinted contacts he stared. "It's too far to hike, even for the likes of you!"

Claire suspended all reaction, not sure what to say.

"Yeah, you've been found out." He drove his face so close that she had to step back. "And don't think I won't be watching."

Claire exhaled heavily in defeat. "I was just asking," she said, hanging her head and looking away.

3

As the Crow Flies

Walking behind Claire, Victor carried a compass to track a northeasterly direction. They were traveling into uncharted territory, a deep wooded valley, miles from Claire's typical scouting grounds. "Keep to your left," Victor said, for what seemed to Claire like the tenth time. "You're veering off course." He wore a red paisley bandanna over his trailing black hair.

Claire turned and stomped her foot. "I know!" Wavelets of white hair framed her perspiring forehead. They stood on a hillside along a narrow deer path cutting through a dense thicket of bramble. "Go left, if you want." She pointed down the hillside covered with blackberry bushes. "But I'm staying out of those stickers."

Victor huffed his annoyance and pulled the bandanna from his silky hair. He stared hard at the image of a black crow stamped on the back of her white tee shirt. The crow, she had said, would be their trip mascot. "You're the one said we should travel 'as the crow flies.'" Squinting at the sun, he stuffed the bandanna into his jeans pocket. "Every time we veer off course, the trip gets longer."

At 10:00 am, they were already three miles from Claire's home. She wore a pedometer on her waist and, as always, binoculars around her neck. And each carried a backpack loaded with provisions. So equipped, the two looked like a team, though physically they could not appear more different. Victor had gained a few inches since the start of the school year (now nearing its close) and stood only two inches shorter than Claire. His growth spurt during the sixth grade was like watching time-lapse video. Conversely, she had grown not one bit, seemingly stalled at 5' 5". What never would change between them, however, was their coloring. The pigment so lustrously expressed in his golden brown skin, dark chocolate eyes, and midnight hair was absent entirely from her canvass. A pigment disorder left her colorless but for strange golden-yellow eyes, and these she chose to hide behind blue-tinted lenses. Only her close family, Jerry, and most recently, Victor, knew the secret of her real eye color.

At the journey's outset, the two friends followed the tame spring-fed brook bordering Claire's yard. Gradually the brook acquired a different character, cutting deeper into a downward sloping terrain, at times plunging into waterfalls of several feet. Climbing over large boulders crowding the creek bed, the two explorers had felt exhilarated. But nearing the creek's confluence with a larger watercourse, they felt tired.

"How many miles have we covered?" Victor asked for the third time in half an hour. He stood atop a hillock, as high as a house, the last in a succession of rolling bulges in the crumpled earth.

"About three miles," she said, huffing with the effort of climbing yet another ridge. "So stop asking!" Whenever

Victor annoyed her, Claire wanted to complain to him about Billy because, despite what he thought, Billy was trouble. Still she hesitated to tell him of her latest encounter with the rude, donkey-faced boy since retelling their exchange would only make Victor mad, especially given their supposed "truce." Too, she felt wicked for not feeling compassion for Billy, whose father was a fugitive from law.

She dropped to her knees within a stand of striped maple covering the hillock like quills of a porcupine. From her backpack she withdrew a newspaper clipping, an article about the return of Robert Crawley. In a photo he stood smiling in front of his impressive stone lodge. "Just look at this place," she said, pointing to two rounded towers, one on either edge of the stone citadel. "Can you believe we'll soon be exploring the grounds? And who knows? Maybe a window or door will be unlocked."

Standing over her, Victor dropped his backpack to the ground. "You don't fool me." He pointed to the boyish-looking man in his mid 30s whose smiling face filled the foreground. "You got a crush on that Crawley guy."

Claire felt herself blush. "You're stupid." She folded the clipping and stuffed it back into her pack. "He's a grown man, older even than my mother!" She popped up off the ground, dragging the backpack in her haste to leave.

"I'm tired and hungry," he called after her. "Let's stop here for a snack."

She took a deep breath, hoping the flush had left her cheeks. Choosing a spot several feet from where he knelt, ruffling inside his pack, she sat cross-legged onto the damp ground. Into the still hot air came the brisk sound of snapping branches. Somewhere below, yet out of sight, a commotion of crackling brushwood drew their eyes. Up the hillside directly toward them bounded a red fox, sleek and silky. Fixed on escape, the fleeing fox did not see the two blocking its way until nearly upon them. The fox then bolted aside, just feet from Victor. Both adventurers turned toward the fox when yet a larger sound—a crush of clumsy progress through brittle undergrowth—drew their eyes again to the hillside.

"That's something big," Victor said to himself before leaping to his feet. "Move!" He swung toward Claire and dove in her direction. Skidding on his chest, he pulled her down by the knees, rolling out from beneath her. Claire rolled with him, one shoulder then the next hitting the ground until stopped by a tree trunk. Crumpled against it, facing opposite the summit, they could not see the two playful bear cubs pursuing the fox. Claire pushed up to catch a last glimpse of the gamboling pair before their hind ends disappeared down the hillside. "How sweet—" she said but Victor groped her head to drive it downward.

"The mother," he whispered, "will be following."

Claire tucked her head inside folded arms, expecting the swipe of a deadly claw or a grip of merciless teeth. Breath suspended, heart racing, she mentally prayed, "Don't let her see us," knowing all the while that their scent couldn't be hidden.

Up the small hill lumbered the mother bear, 275 pounds of lean muscle, her body fat dissipated by a winter of hibernation and springtime of nursing young. Yet a season of berries would soon sustain her, though for now her stomach was filled with grubs found under rocks and boulders. The fox did not interest the mother other than as the subject of her cubs' frolic. Attending to their safety, she followed behind.

The human scent was one the bear knew well since it signaled danger. Sensing it, she quickened her pace to a trot, intent on discerning whether the scent trails—her cubs and the humans—converged. If so, the danger was immediate. The bear crested the hill, plunging into a current of foul human odor while the sweet scent of her cubs flowed to the left. She followed their trail, preparing to lead her cubs to safety up a huge white pine.

"It's okay," Victor said, pushing upward. "The bear's gone."

"Didn't she smell us?" Claire sounded a bit disappointed but relieved.

"Oh, she smelled us all right." Victor hopped to his feet. "But why start a fight if you don't have to?" He brushed the dirt from his palms onto his jeans. Victor knew a lot about black bears; in fact, his Cochiti name was Black Bear, in the language of Keres, *Muh'nah'kain Kuhaia*. Only recently had he shared his Native American name with Claire, though

months earlier giving her one that meant "Moon Woman"—
Tahwach K'uyow.

Invigorated with their wild animal sightings, they raced alongside the creek eager to find its intersection with a small river. The topographical map Victor had taken from his father's office showed a flat floodplain before the creek met the river. Since they were already at the lowest elevation, the confluence must be directly ahead. This joining was heard before seen—an amplified whisper of rolling waters.

"I hear it," Victor called to Claire, who had stopped to aim her binoculars high in a red pine on a beautiful male Blackburnian Warbler, the only warbler with a brilliant orange throat. But it flitted away before she could focus.

"I'm coming," she called back, stumbling into a small ground hole and nearly twisting her ankle.

"Hurry up—I see it!"

Claire hobbled quickly along, testing her ankle and scanning the uneven, rocky ground for additional surprises. And when at last she raised her eyes from the ground, she saw it, too: a lustrous, rolling force of nature. She rushed to stand alongside Victor, who stood at the edge of an open wedge of land where the two waters met. Together they watched the swift crystalline waters embrace the tranquil flow of the spring-fed creek and carry it away.

Delighted, they rooted themselves to the spot for lunch. Kneeling in soft matted grasses, Victor searched his backpack for a sandwich of avocado and butter. He then exchanged half for Claire's cucumber and cream cheese, a bargain made earlier. "Not bad," he said, one cheek stuffed full, "but I like my avocado better." Hungrily they ate until stomachs relenting, they took time to talk. "Does it worry you," Victor took a swig of water from his canteen, "that Clyde Hollow might still be in these woods?"

Mention of Billy's father made Claire cringe. "Don't say that," she scolded, rising up on bended knees to rearrange her long bare legs. Sitting cross-legged, she bent forward to say emphatically, "Hollow is long gone. Jerry says so and the police, too."

"How do they know for sure?" he challenged. "Hollow could be watching us right now." He comically shifted his smiling eyes side to side. Claire playfully poked his leg with her foot, which he grabbed. "Stop poking me or I'll drag you into the water." She laughed as he stood to pull her along, both knowing he wouldn't dare. Nor could he with her other foot poised for a powerful punch. Giggling, he collapsed beside her and tentatively they ventured into the subject that caused Claire such discomfort—the day Clyde Hollow had held her, him, Billy, and Sammy as hostages at gunpoint.

She and Victor had been sent on a mission to retrieve Jerry's homing pigeon, Patty, from his cabin in the woods. Slow to learn her new address at the country store, Patty persisted in flying "home" to Jerry's woodland cabin. But they arrived to find that the pigeon was not alone. Clyde Hollow, drunk and deranged, was using Jerry's cabin as his personal hunting camp, intending to teach his reluctant son Billy how to shoot. Being discovered in this trespass by two indignant adolescents did not bother Hollow. Instead, brandishing a rifle, he chose to lecture the juveniles, especially Billy, on their disgraceful disrespect.

Any drunkard with a gun was a volatile mix, so at first opportunity the young hostages, including Billy, escaped into the woods. Later that evening, at the cabin, police found no trace of Clyde Hollow, who then became a fugitive from law.

"There go your mascots," said Victor, as a large flock of noisy crows flew overhead. Yet he spoke too soon because this band of rough, tough, shiny black birds dropped from the sky to land within the canopies of surrounding red oaks. Mewing like cats, bleating like sheep, and making all manner of bizarre sounds, the raucous band seemed intent on investigating them.

A single black crow descended through the trees to perch on a branch directly above Claire. She threw a chunk of blueberry muffin to the ground and the crow swooped down beside the fast running creek to eat it. Then on sturdy, feathered legs it waddled toward Claire, asking for more.

"I can't believe it," Victor said with a full mouth. "It's not afraid of you."

"Why should it be?" she countered, throwing another chunk of muffin. "These are intelligent birds. Probably a local band that knows me."

27

Victor sometimes thought Claire pretentious, as with this ridiculous claim. "Those birds don't know you." He twisted a grin and rolled his eyes.

"Why couldn't they know me?" she said self-importantly. "I'm in the woods a lot. Besides, crows keep track of people's comings and goings." In truth, she suspected that the crows did know *her* personally; she was, after all, special to the birds. And this reality sustained her whenever self-conscious about her appearance. "Are you this band's leader?" Claire asked the shiny blue-black bird cocking its head. The crow cawed, flapped and then folded his wings before diving toward the largest morsel yet thrown.

Victor was becoming unnerved by the heightening noise of the watching crows. One to the other they incessantly called in high nasal tones that were grating to his ears.

"Victor!" she cried. "This crow has a white patch on his shoulder. Let's name him!" Victor stood to quickly charge at the bird that flew directly over his head and into the trees above. "Why did you do that?" she demanded as a dozen crows took flight, swallowing his grumbled response in their swell of beating black wings. "What did you just say?"

"Let's go, Tahwach."

Claire was certain he had said something else entirely, but whenever he called her Tahwach, she couldn't stay mad. "I'll name the crow myself," she said, indignantly, hoisting her backpack. Following Victor as he traced a path alongside the river, she announced, "Colonel White Badge."

The terrain beside the river was level, populated by a host of yellow birch. The still hot air felt oppressive; even the birds had quieted under its weight. For some time they traveled in silence, Victor brooding over Claire's self-important attitude. Indulging in a thorough examination of her failings, he finally relented, thinking himself too harsh when Claire broke the silence.

"It's strange that Robert Crawley and the others haven't been able to find that Ivory-billed Woodpecker," she mused. Of course, it would come to me, if only I could get down to Arkansas."

Victor stopped, turned, and announced that they were heading back. Since his mood had turned foul, Claire decided not to argue. Besides, she too was tiring. "Okay. But you don't have to be nasty." She quickly turned to follow, feeling suddenly vulnerable, as if someone hidden might be watching.

4

Taking a Leap

Seated at his bedroom desk before a computer screen, Victor surveyed a satellite image of the land between Claire's property and Crawley's lodge. Outside the night pressed against his window, slightly opened to an evening breeze that carried the scent of a nearby skunk. Illuminated on the computer screen was a knobby, rippling carpet of green. A spot of bald earth surrounded by woodland marked the billionaire's retreat.

Aerial photographs revealed a forest different than the maze of trees through which they had rambled on their first unplanned trek. Now he saw a green mantle, shaped like a continent, its borders ragged and chewed by devouring farmlands. And beyond these farmlands were towns, islands of densely packed houses intersected by roads. But most interesting was the location of the turreted retreat, which sat no more than two miles from the woodland's eastern border. Entering here, they could quickly reach it.

Victor closed the lid to his laptop, just as his mother pounded on the bedroom door. "It's past midnight," she said in a harried voice. "Would you pl-e-e-e-a-s-e go to sleep!"

"I'm going!" He plopped heavily, face down, onto his single bed to make it squeal.

"And make sure you stay there!"

Victor pulled a fleece blanket over his head to hide from his mother's nagging, which seemed to him an entity in itself—a living, breathing badger burrowing in his mother's mind. Sometimes he imagined the weasel-like animal riding on her shoulder, whispering words into her ear.

Victor didn't need a degree in psychology to realize his mother had become growingly obsessive and paranoid about his wellbeing. In fact, she so feared for his safety that he wasn't allowed out of the house when she was absent from it. Even now she paced behind his door, unwilling to abandon her post until he turned off the light. He reached for the pull string of the bedside lamp and clicked it off.

He punched the pillow before burying his face, leaking tears into it. His father had promised she would get better; that the cloud over her spirit would pass and she would again shine. But already years had past. Victor needed to believe that his *real* mother—the person with deep chestnut hair rolling in waves onto her shoulder—would emerge from the impostor who wore short, bleached hair with dark roots. Often he stared at those roots, clinging to the remnants of what had been.

* * *

In the light of dawn, Victor's father stood facing east at the edge of an expansive lake, still and dark. The sun hid below the horizon of forest crowding the opposite shore. The smell

31

of water, deep with life and decay, quenched his senses. From a small suede pouch he pinched a measure of cornmeal and sprinkled it into the air as he prayed aloud in his Pueblo language. He thanked the Creator for the world and its creatures and offered his grandmother and grandfather spirits the food of cornmeal. Feeding his ancestral spirits sustained them in the next world.

After his prayer, he stood quietly, breathing in the morning air. How he wished his estranged wife Rose was standing beside him, enjoying the earthy smells of the coming summer. He prayed now for her health because she was not well.

He scanned for waterfowl on the lake, its surface polished by the growing light. A flock huddled against the far shore was too distant to distinguish. But he saw an approaching pair winging their way up the lake and toward him. From their silhouette against the bluing sky, he knew them to be a pair of Wood Ducks. Smiling, he watched them land in the water just beyond the shore.

As a wildlife conservation officer, George Arquetana knew the status of the animals he protected. That the population of this colorful duck species was stable and increasing made him glad. With a lighter heart he headed back to the cabin to prepare for a morning appointment with local law enforcement. Officer Mahone wanted to discuss a citizen's complaint of a deer poacher.

* * *

The next morning, with the sound of his mother's departing car, Victor prepared his escape. Though Friday, school was closed for a teacher's in-service day and he and Claire had the day to themselves. Leaving the house unnoticed wasn't easy with nosey neighbors, especially the old woman across the street. Though ancient, Lillian wore flaming orange hair, like a clown, and rose-red lipstick. All day long she sat crumpled in decrepitude before her front window, gulping with greedy eyes all that she could see. Victor hurriedly called Claire, telling her to meet him on bicycle halfway to his house.

"No, Victor!" she half shouted, half whined. "You said we could try for the Crawley lodge again."

"We are!" he said. "I found a shortcut, but we have to get there by bike. I'll see you in 15 minutes." He disconnected before she could respond.

Victor needed to dash unseen across the backyard to his bike hidden within a stand of spruce. To fool the neighbors, enlisted as spies on his mother's behalf, he stuffed his long black hair into a baseball cap and placed a small CD player in his open window, the volume high enough to be heard but not to annoy. Then through his living room window he watched Lillian, awaiting his chance. It came immediately, when a package delivery truck pulled up to her front yard. Victor flew out the kitchen door and into the trees, not believing his luck. Peddling fast, he followed a bumpy path through a wooded strip, flooded with pools of late morning sun. Soon his tires were rolling onto macadam, heading down Kelly Store Road.

Victor slowed to rip off his hair-stuffed cap before taking the bend in the road, behind which he expected to find Claire. Blood pumping, grinning in expectation, he took the curve. And there, astride her bike at the entrance of a long dirt lane bordering a woodland, waited Claire, her white hair radiant in the strong morning light.

Though smiling, she opened with a complaint. "I waited for your call all morning," she said, one long leg anchored to the ground, the other about to pump a pedal.

"Mom's shift was changed." He directed his bike onto the dirt lane edging an open field. "She's working lunch and dinner today." Victor speeded ahead to practice a wheelie, but the bike slipped from beneath him, his feet hitting the ground in a run. Mounting again, he said, "Let's go!"

Over rutted pasture tracks and hard roads they pedaled, picking their way through creek beds and thickets, and at times climbing fences over which they hoisted their bikes, until reaching their entrance point into the woods. Jumping off his bike, Victor checked his watch. "It's been an hour. How many miles did we cover?"

But Claire's attention was elsewhere. Scooting off the seat, she gently laid down the bike, head cocked, listening. "Hear that?"

Through the background hum of insects he could hear a bird's chattering. "Yeah, some bird hidden in the grass."

"But do you know what kind?" She twisted toward him,

snowy brows arched in doubt. A sweet smell of honeysuckle surrounded her.

The challenge amused Victor. He grinned while she waited for his admission of ignorance. "I'll bet half your lunch it's the bird on your shirt." He walked toward her, nodding at the appliqué on her tee shirt of a bird with bright yellow under parts and a black V-shaped bib. "So am I right?"

She shook her head, lips pinched to keep from smiling. "Even so, you don't *know* the bird."

"I do now." Up from the mounded grass flew a flash of bright yellow—a feathered missile winging past to perch on a nearby maple sapling. The lanky meadow bird hopped from a branch bouncing beneath its weight to a sturdier limb with glossy leaves. Then to the sky he raised his throat rolling with a wellspring of perfect sound.

"I know that song!" he gushed. "It's an Eastern Meadowlark. I heard it with my father. Listen." And he whistled the brilliant notes of birdsong.

Claire gaped, astonished at the fidelity of his replication. "Victor, he's in your heart!"

"You think?" Dark eyes gleaming with delight and mischief, he said, "So if I wear birds on my shirt, they'll come flocking to me, just like for you?"

"Because it works for me," she said, voice suddenly aloof, "doesn't mean it will for you." They studied the bird through binoculars until it dove within the waiting grasses. "And I wish you wouldn't talk about it— "

"You brought it up!" He nearly stepped on her heels as she turned away. "And why shouldn't we talk about it?"

She twisted toward him but avoided his eyes. "Because talking about it seems like betraying their trust somehow. It was our secret—the birds and mine—until I told you."

"You told Jerry before you told me," he charged.

"Well that was different." She turned away. "It slipped out. Besides, Jerry explained about the birds in my heart. Until then I didn't understand how I drew them to me. How my deep love for birds attracts them."

The mid-day sun flashed off the chrome of their bicycles. Claire hoisted hers from the ground to push into the shaded woodland. Victor followed. Inside they concealed their bikes beneath the thorny branches of a drooping barberry. The two-mile hike to Crawley's lodge would be on foot. They walked through a corridor of wild rye, a brush of gold creeping into the woods from the pasture over an old logging road. Claire ahead and Victor behind, they scanned the emerald woodland. A touch of fragrant wind scattered the sunlight and set the trees to shimmer. The meadowlark's plaintive song followed them.

"Does the meadowlark's song sound sad to you?" she asked.

"Not sad so much . . ." He stopped to listen. "More like he's longing for something. And you know what I long for?" he asked in a teasing, tempting way? "Food!"

Claire giggled, dropping to her knees beside him to unpack

their luncheon. Taking a bite from her peanut butter and jelly sandwich, she watched Victor unwrap his, waiting to see if he would first feed his grandmother and grandfather spirits before taking a bite. Victor's father had explained the ritual on a visit to their store. Before taking a sip of coffee, he had touched the surface of the hot beverage with his fingertip, a drop being adequate to sustain those living in the spiritual realm.

As Claire feigned inattention, Victor obliged by pinching a piece of the crust, then lowering it into the grass. Consuming their sandwiches, they hopped up, Claire clutching an apple in her teeth and Victor gulping water from his canteen. He grabbed her backpack to sling onto his back. "I owe you for lunch."

Heading due west, they followed an old logging corridor, now a woodland lane trimmed in ox-eye daisies. They drifted along, attentive to the air woven with birdsong until the terrain began to buckle and grow rocky. Soon they were descending into cooler air, sweetened by the scent of running water, hidden by a long, sinuous column of waxy-leafed rhododendron. Downward toward the creek they skidded and stumbled, laughing with the thrill. Spanning the creek was a fallen red oak over which they crossed. Gripped by a sense of urgency, they scaled upward from the hollow.

"How much farther?" Claire asked, legs tiring.

Victor took a breath and glanced at his compass. "What's your pedometer reading?"

"Look!" She pointed to something in the far distance on a

rise above them. "A turret!" High above the living green canopy of trees thrust a white limestone tower. Its pointed orange roof of ceramic tile pierced the blue sky.

"I told you!" Claire cried, charging off as if in a race. He pursued, passing her on their angled ascent along the ridge with quicker, surer footing. The climb upward grew steeper until it rose before them almost as a wall to be scaled. Victor began the assent, pulling himself upward by the base of sapling trees and then using these like rungs in a ladder. Claire followed behind until into her upward looking face earth sprayed from the traction of his boots.

"Watch it!" she yelled, blinking to dislodge dirt from her eyes.

"I didn't mean to," he said. "Are you okay?"

One hand clutching an exposed rope-like root, Claire scoured the precipice with the other searching for something to grab. "I can't climb any higher, Victor. It's too steep."

"Sure you can," he said. "The top is right above me."

His boot, which had provided her some comfort in its proximity, disappeared and she felt a surge of panic. She pressed her cheek against the crumbling wall of earth, root, and tangled vine. Her breath became a pant, apace with her quickening heart. "Victor!" she cried. "I can't move."

Squatting above on solid, horizontal ground, Victor looked down to Claire. "Don't worry," he said, flopping on his stomach to reach an arm over the edge. "Grab my hand and I'll help pull you up."

Once atop, she spared a single glance over the edge to see what they had risked. "We're not going back this way," she said, brushing dirt from her hands as she stood. Toward their long-sought objective they both now turned, hoping to see the turreted chateau, modeled after those of 15th-century France. But instead they faced a six-foot stone and mortar wall.

"What?" Claire shouted at Victor, as if this new barrier were his fault. "Who builds a wall around a stupid lodge hidden in the woods?"

"I guess your hero Robert Crawley does," Victor said, snickering.

Not amused, she demanded, "Didn't you see this wall in *your* satellite images?"

He countered, "Didn't you read about it in *your* Crawley article?"

"Oooohhh!" She slapped arms heavily to her sides, stomping off to follow the seemingly endless wall.

"What are you doing?" he called after.

Arms flung in exasperation, she cried, "What else? Looking for an entrance."

"I think I found one." He looked up into a large, sprawling maple tree.

She charged over the corridor separating the wall from the woodland and its precipice. "We can't scale that wall—"

"We don't have to." He nodded to the tree whose broad sturdy limbs reached well over and above the wall. Claire needed no further inducements. Clutching a limb with a slight jump, she swung her legs up to a fork, threading through one long leg. Strong and agile, she hoisted herself upward and straddled the split trunk, deeply inhaling a wafting scent of lilac. She smiled down at Victor, confident once again.

"Better move out of the way," he said, eager for the satisfaction. "I'm coming up." He leapt to clutch the same limb but missed.

"Take off the backpacks," coached Claire. "We'll get them when we leave."

Victor dropped the excess baggage and tried again but missed. "Wait!" he cried. "I got an idea."

Curious, Claire watched as he emptied his backpack of its remaining contents, lining these against the wall. Focused on his curious activity, she didn't give thought to the swell of birdsong brimming over the stone barricade. Then a heavy current of sweet scent—roses—yanked her senses awake, and turning toward its source, she looked for the first time to what lie within the wall. The sight dazzled her: a flowing landscape erupting everywhere with color and scent.

Bold red and yellow rose bushes bordered a meandering path that opened onto islands of mutinous flowers in a cultivated green sea. Ornamental trees in fragrant blossom filled the air with purple, pink, and white clouds. Claire climbed up onto a broad bough of the tree, eager to see more, while below Victor swung the canvas backpack up and over the limb that eluded his grasp.

"What do you see?" he called up to her.

"You won't believe it!" She crouched to scoot along the bough, grasping a higher, parallel branch for support. Its leaves shook in distress. She could look directly over the wall to a tangle of black raspberry vines crowding its stone face.

"If we jump from here," she called to Victor, who now swung from the lower limb by the straps of the backpack slung over it, "we'll have to clear these raspberries." Victor could only grunt, his feet a scuttle against the trunk. But when next she looked, he had squirmed his way up into the fork.

"I could sure use a drink of water," he said, huffing, looking regretfully at the canteen leaning against the wall below.

"Victor, would you get over here!" she said impatiently. At the farthest point possible on the broad bough she still squat, devising a method for descending. Beyond, the sturdy limb tapered and diverged into smaller branches, and directly below awaited the tabletop surface of the stone wall. She lowered herself onto it as Victor stepped out onto the bough.

His response to the view was an extended two-note whistle.

"Isn't it fantastic!" Claire gushed. But Victor made no response, set entirely on groping his way along the tree limb toward the wall. Only when he stood alongside her atop it, did he finally comment.

"Like paradise."

A welcoming committee of four Ruby-throated Hummingbirds abruptly arrived, buzzing about the newcomers, frantic to surround them. After several orbits and much squeaky twittering, the tiny iridescent birds decided on a square formation, hovering eye-level with Victor and Claire.

"Are they studying us?" Victor asked, delighted by these fantastical creatures. The males' ruby throats seemed to flash on and off.

"Seems so," Claire said, choosing one to address: "Nice garden. Mind if we take a look?"

Orbiting their guest a final time, the committee of four flew swiftly into the garden. Victor and Claire exchanged one look, bent their knees, and jumped.

5

Hollow's Hideout

"Nice jump," Victor said of Claire's technique as he bounced from the ground. Brushing a tangle of black hair from his face, he looked behind to the vines of raspberries. "These are ripe!" he cried, starting to gather the juicy berries.

"Not now!" Claire said.

"But I'm thirsty."

She grunted in disapproval and dashed off without him through the overgrown lawn. Torn between the gorgeous flowers and the chateau, Claire sputtered over the ground. She dove her nose into a sumptuous pink peony and swam in its scent, only to be pulled onward by the shining turrets with orange roofs.

She trotted slowly through the rose-bordered path. It meandered across the upward sloping grounds. Everywhere on mounded islands, small and large, was a blur of intoxicating flowers—heaps and spikes and spires of flowers, blushing or screaming with color. And these hosted many more hummingbirds, electrifying the air with the sound of their high-voltage wings. When she again stopped, to marvel at giant snapdragons, Victor sneaked up from behind, his grin tinted purple from raspberries.

"Hey!"

She jumped. "What took you so long?"

Chapter 5

"Here!" He held out his baseball cap, serving as a bowl for raspberries. "I brought you some." A fistful went immediately into her mouth and the tiny birds once again drew near. "Have you ever seen so many hummingbirds?" Victor said, astonished. Dozens dotted the air, dipping and rising among the flowers.

"It's incredible," she said, rotating to take it all in. "Hey, what's that?" Just below the chateau, hidden by low, creamy clouds of late-blooming dogwood trees, something flashed in the sun. Claire darted from the island of snapdragons to cross the grounds diagonally. Victor chased behind, clutching the cap with its precious berries. Through shaggy grass they ran upward toward a grove of young Japanese Dogwood, trees as wide as they were tall. Ahead, she saw an opening within the grove.

"I hear a fountain!" She sprinted toward the clearing and then into what seemed an outside room with the sky for ceiling. The area was totally private, enclosed by a rounded ring of the dogwood. At the far end rose a limestone wall built into a high, long bank of earth. And from some hidden source among its rocks bubbled water, sliding over a rock terrace into a pool below. Claire gawked at the engineered wonder, unaware of Victor until he became part of the scene, kneeling before the wall by the large, shallow pond.

"Don't drink that!" she shouted, as he scooped a handful of water.

"It smells fine," he said, taking a sip. "Look at those Japanese Koi." He pointed to a half dozen fish swimming up to them. White as cream with bright orange markings they reminded Claire of large, exotic goldfish. While she studied them, Victor surveyed the opposite bank covered with periwinkle, blue-violet flowers woven within an evergreen carpet. It spread outward from the pond to a stone walkway.

"Look!" Victor said, popping up. "There's a stone stairway over there." He took a few steps backward to get a better perspective and tripped on a stair behind him. "Hey. Stairs are on this side, too. They lead up to the top of the wall."

They both dashed up the stone steps, which wound leftward up the bank. "Wait!" Claire halted, eyes wide. "I'll go up the other stairs and we'll meet at the top!"

"Okay, but hurry."

Spinning on heels, pumping arms, she sprang away to trace the pond, shaped like a squashed circle. Within the water, the koi followed her feet like iron to magnet. At the base of the rightward winding steps, she shouted "Okay" and both bounded up the wide stone flight. They reached the top together on opposite sides of a patio paved with yellow clay bricks. These swirled in a circle toward a central point which, like a whirlpool, drew them inward to gape up at what sprouted from its center: a glistening white marble sculpture.

Mouths gaping, they looked to one another and then back, tracing the sculpture with their eyes from base to top. It grew

45

in the likeness of a tree that climbed above their heads before extending a strong lateral limb onto which a raptor descended—claws rooting to bark; legs bracing and wide; wings sweeping upward; tail broadly fanning. The huge hawk peered down with fierce eyes.

"It's a Red-tail," said Victor, pointing to the rose marble of the hawk's tail. The sculpture otherwise was entirely white.

"It's Ku-Khain," said Claire.

Her simple observation broke the spell as Victor hastened to disagree. "No it's not," he said, dismissing the obvious exaggeration. "With you everything is some bigger deal than it really is."

"You don't think this is a big deal," she said, looking up into the hawk's face.

"You know what I mean." Victor paced opposite of Claire to look at the sculpture from another angle. "Just because it's a hawk doesn't mean it's Big Red. Not everyone is obsessed like you."

"Her name is now Ku-Khain," Claire reminded him with reprimand. "And why else would there be a cross on her chest?" Victor sought the spot to which she pointed. The white marble of the hawk's breast contained color like that of the tail but much lighter.

"That's just a color in the stone," Victor pronounced. "Besides it's an X, not a cross."

"I know it's a color in the stone," she said flippantly. "But why is it on her chest?"

"Just coincidence."

"Sure. I believe that," she said, rolling her eyes at his stupidity. She circled the statue, gesturing broadly. "This entire sculpture is totally white *except* for the tail and the cross on her breast—"

"I don't care." Victor turned toward the chateau. "I'm not standing here all day." Claire followed, heaving an exasperated sigh. They headed toward a second patio, about head-level above them. Yellow brick stairs led to this upper rectangular terrace, bordered by a low brick wall. Ornate benches and planters dotted the courtyard, but neither could attend to these with their goal now within reach. Hurrying through a stone archway, they were at last to the chateau itself!

A wide walkway outlined the back of the stone building, rectangular but for fat round towers bulging from either end. It was to the left tower Claire raced, not once stopping to peer into the windows she passed. Victor, however, had not moved from the first such window encountered. It was tall and arched, with casement windows that could be swung open like a door. Hands cupped to glass, he looked inside.

"It's the kitchen!" he shouted, but Claire had other interests. She paced the swell of white limestone that was the tower, eager to locate a window into which she could see. But even the lowest of these long, narrow openings were just above her head. She snorted in frustration. "I can't see in!"

47

she hollered, looking now to Victor, who still hung outside the kitchen window.

"Well come down here," he called back. "I can see plenty."

Sulking, she stomped away from her prized turret, glancing with seeming disinterest into the first window and the view within that made her gawk.

"What?" Victor cried, running to close the distance between them. "What is it?" He cupped both hands to the glass, bolting his eyes into place. Inside a spacious room of overstuffed couches and chairs, white pedestals of various heights grew from a shiny oak floor. Atop these pedestals perched life-sized statutes of birds, painted to replicate their flesh and blood counterparts.

"Victor, look!" Claire said, her high forehead pressed against the glass. "That's a Northern Shrike."

"Which one?"

"And a Redpoll and a Purple Finch and a Brown Creeper and a Horned Lark—"

"Stop!" Victor said. "You're going too fast! Which is the— what did you call it—a strike?"

But Claire ignored him, lost in her excitement. "And look—a Ruby-crowned Kinglet. I love them."

"Where?" Victor nearly screamed with frustration.

"That tiny bird, with the red cap. It's on the column beside the pale yellow loveseat. See the white circle around its eye?"

"How can you see that from here?" Victor complained. "It's too far away."

"I can see it fine. You just don't know these birds and I do."

Victor changed the subject. He didn't like her know-it-all attitude. "I wonder if he's got statues in every room. I bet there's a couple dozen right here." Intruding on their reverie came the sound of an engine. Distant and hollow, the sound did not at first draw their attention. But as it grew nearer, gaining substance, both friends cocked their heads. As the blasting engine grew louder, alarm flooded their faces.

"Someone's coming," squealed Claire. "We've got to hide!" Victor grabbed her wrist, pulling her toward the tower to their left. She was surprised at the strength of his grip and tugged at her arm to release it. "Not that way," she hissed. "They'll see us!"

"They won't. Trust me." And he yanked her back to his side, once again towing her behind. She let herself be drawn around the tower and toward the chateau's side. There, to her relief, grew a row of rhododendron in full bloom. Planted a few feet from the building, the high shrubs provided cover. Claire felt safe hidden behind the tangle of stems and long, leathery leaves. But Victor kept pushing on toward the front of the chateau, his grip about her wrist tightening with the tension of the growing noise.

"Come on," he shouted over the engine screaming in front of the chateau. Before Claire could respond, the rider switched off the ignition; all became quiet except for the

Chapter 5

bumble of hairy bees grazing on fat purple flowers. She instantly broke Victor's loosened grip and backed against the wall. To his beseeching look, she shook her head, "no."

Turning away, Victor slid his back against the cool stones following an outstretched arm. Only feet from the corner, he could hear the rider dismount and the crunch of footfalls over loose gravel. As the sound retreated, Victor peered from around the corner. He did not expect whom he saw and spoke the name aloud: "Billy."

Claire sprang upward. She could see Victor stepping out from the corner, raising an arm in greeting, about to call out—

"No!" she commanded.

Victor swung his head sideways to look at her. She dropped to her knees, clasping her hands theatrically. This time she would plead, anything to divert his attention from calling out to Billy.

It worked.

Victor looked ahead, hesitated, and then looked back at her. "What are you doing?" he said, ducking back into the cover of woody shrub. "It's just Billy. He's probably come to find us."

"Did you tell him we'd be here?" she cried, groping the wall to stand.

"No. I haven't even seen him."

"Then why is he here?"

"Let's just ask him." Victor turned but Claire grabbed his arm.

"Won't you listen for a second?" A flower dipping beside her hair cast it with a purple tint. He took a deep breath to calm his agitation and took in the sultry, sweet fragrance of the petal's oils. His dark brown eyes softened and then shifted in thought.

"Why do you wear those colored contacts when you're with me? I prefer your own golden eyes."

Claire lowered these, a feather-touch of white lashes against pale skin. "But what if we ran into someone?"

Victor understood. When out in the world, she'd never risk someone seeing her honey-amber eyes, though he thought them beautiful. "So what do you want to do?"

"Let's be quiet, so we can hear what he's doing." She pointed to the front of the building, indicating that they should move toward it. A confused bumblebee flew from a flower into Claire's hair. Waving it away, she felt something flimsy fall onto her upraised hand. She pulled it down to her face. It was a piece of cellophane, like a wrapper around a pack of cigarettes. Confused, she looked upward and smelled cigarette smoke. Then voices floated on the air. She reached blindly for Victor, already beyond her grasp. If she could hear *them*, then they could also hear. She stumbled ahead and bumped into Victor, who was also looking up. He put a finger to his lips and they both listened.

"I told you not to bring that four-wheeler inside the gate," said a man in a low, throaty voice.

"Yeah. I forgot."

"Are you a fool?" The man coughed up phlegm from his chest and spit it out over the balcony. The eavesdropping pair below grimaced with disgust. "You're leaving tracks directly to me!"

"Okay, I get it," Billy whined.

Victor and Claire gaped at one another; the second speaker was Billy. At once, they both understood: Clyde Hollow, Billy's father and a fugitive from the law, was standing on a balcony above their heads.

"Huh!" Clyde puffed heavily from his cigarette. "No one's supposed to be here. When you leave, I'll have to sweep away those tracks."

As father and son spoke, Victor and Claire learned of the situation. Clyde Hollow had been hiding out at Robert Crawley's chateau ever since the old caretaker had been hospitalized two weeks earlier. And Billy had become his "runner," bringing in supplies, like cigarettes, and other necessities not already available in the billionaire's well-stocked pantry or liquor cabinets.

When the outlaws finally headed in doors from the balcony, Claire and Victor dashed madly to retrace their steps through the terraced patios. Once concealed within the flowering dogwood grove, they stopped to catch their breath.

"I could sure use a drink of water," lamented Victor.

Under an umbrella of low-hanging branches, Claire found his abandoned cap, still half full with berries. He took it from her eagerly. Slumping to the ground, his face contorted into a grimace.

"What?" she demanded.

"The wall," he said, gloomily. "We jumped down into the garden. How are we going to get back up?"

The only solution was to leave unseen by the front gate, but would it be open? And how could they cross so much territory unseen? Hidden in the grove of dogwood trees, they were blind to Clyde and Billy's whereabouts inside the chateau. For too long they fretted over these questions because the sound of a four-wheeler revving to life caught them totally off guard. In a panic they darted from their hiding place to dash across open grounds toward the limestone wall. Against it they crouched, waiting for Billy to pull out ahead, hoping to follow undetected behind.

6

New Day for Moon Doggy

Air thick with exhaust, Claire and Victor slipped unseen through the black-iron gate behind Billy and his blasting four-wheeler. Victor led the retreat outside the front wall with Claire stepping on his heels. "We have to tell the police!" Claire cried from behind, trying to take the lead. "Hollow is dangerous!"

Seeing the corner, Victor began to run. "He's nothing but a drunk." Claire felt she must beat him to prove something and overtook his stride with her longer legs. Careening around the corner of the back wall, she overshot the maple and skidded to a stop, turning to trot back as Victor stooped to grab the canteen propped against the wall. Breathing heavily, watching him take a long drink, she said, "You don't fool me."

He wiped the water from his mouth and handed her the canteen, his eyes interested but attitude indifferent. She took a swig. "You don't want Billy angry with you because the Mars mission is about to restart." She referred to the role playing video game *Flight Fever*, wherein Victor and Billy were crew members on a mission to Mars.

His brown eyes glinted like glass. He grabbed the canteen from her hand and ripped the daypack from the ground. "You think you know everything," he said, stuffing it into the pack. "I don't rat out my friends."

"So Clyde Hollow's your friend?" she shouted. He shook his head against the absurd accusation, not to be baited. She stuck her face into his. "We'll just let Robert Crawley stumble into Clyde—is that your plan?"

"I never said that!" Victor marched roughly past her looking for a place to re-enter the woods. Where tall white pines crowded a steep bank, he plunged toward the nearest trunk, wedging himself between the pitching ground and vertical trunk. As she skidded on pine needles toward him, he rolled from the trunk and fell toward the next, bouncing from tree to tree, pinball fashion, shrieking with the thrill of the downhill fall.

Too exhilarated to remain grumpy, the pair spoke less heatedly. Victor explained that telling on Clyde meant that they must confess to trespassing. And no good could come of that. He would be forever grounded and she might never be allowed alone again in the woods. On the rocky spine of a hill, he grabbed a stick to prod a large heap of scat that looked like dehydrated berry preserves. "Bear," he said, tossing the stick aside. "Not only that—" he looked at her with serious, steady eyes, "—what if Billy got charged for helping a fugitive?"

Claire whined into the air. "But what about Robert? We can't just let him walk in on Clyde."

Victor's simple solution was to tell Billy about the billionaire's upcoming visit since he and his father obviously didn't know. "Then Billy will tell Clyde, who will run off like

55

a coward, leaving a fresh trail for the police."

Claire bit her bottom lip in thought. "I suppose so," she said, doubtfully, "if you're certain Billy will tell Clyde in time before Crawley arrives."

Victor grabbed and lifted Claire inches from the ground. "Trust me, Tawach. I'll handle it." A geyser of blood flooded her face as she twisted and dropped from his grasp to stumble ahead.

Later that day, Claire found eating difficult. Anxiety about Clyde Hollow hiding out at the chateau filled her stomach, allowing no room for food. She sat with her mother in the "real" kitchen, a small square room with pale yellow walls and two windows, pretending to sip her mushroom soup. Sammy lay taking a nap on the cool linoleum floor of the adjacent summer kitchen, where in earlier days women canned their vegetables and meats over hot wood-burning stoves during the growing season. More an enclosed porch than a room, it ran behind the storeroom, its outer wall a row of windows, all open to a summer breeze.

Louise didn't notice her daughter's excessive soup stirring, preoccupied with something unpleasant. "I got a letter from mother today," she said, pausing with a slight sigh. "She says Mamo is not well."

Claire's grandmother and great-grandmother, whom she called "Mamo," lived together in County Limerick, Ireland.

"What's wrong with her?" Claire said, dropping her spoon into the soup.

"It's her mind. Mother thinks she's slipping."

Sharing a deep, emotional connection to her great-grandmother, Claire took great offense. "There's nothing wrong with Mamo's mind! I would know; she writes me every month."

"Control yourself, Claire," her mother said, rising from the table to go to the stove, where she ladled soup into a bowl for Jerry, then working in the store. "It might be some passing distraction. At times, your great-grandmother dives too deeply into her interest in Celtic mythology."

"But I love Mamo's stories."

Holding a full bowl to take into Jerry, she said, "So do I, but mother thinks Mamo is losing herself in those stories. She's worried and wants us to visit. I just don't know how."

Claire jettisoned upward, nearly knocking over the chair. "To Ireland? For real?" She had never been to Ireland, a place as magical as the faeries and "good people" of her great-grandmother's stories.

Louise backed away from the whirlwind that was her daughter. "If you make me spill this, Claire, I swear ..." she said, turning just in time to step up into the living room.

After washing the dishes, Claire vented her excitement and anxieties wrestling with Sammy by the pond. Rolling over freshly mowed grass, she squeezed her head between upraised elbows trying to avoid his insistent tongue. Even so, the dog's wet, soggy muzzle sought and found the nape of her neck. "Ahhhhh! I give up," she squealed, jumping to her feet, blades of grass plastered to her back.

"Wait till you hear!" Jerry yelled from across the yard. Face lit with joy, he peddled the ground like a fast walker, arms pumping, hips swaying. On each shoulder perched a bird, fluttering to keep balance. Sammy bounded toward the trio, eager to smell the chicken flapping to the ground. Patty the pigeon did not trust the canine and flew into the locust tree.

"What is it?" Claire called, stumbling over her feet to meet him beneath the tree.

Jerry took a deep breath. Behind a veil of emotion his hazel eyes looked luminous. "You won't believe it."

"Tell me!" She trampled the ground impatiently.

"Helen is giving me Moon Doggy."

"What!"

"She just left the store to get him ready."

Claire grabbed Jerry's hands, jumping up and down. "I can't believe it; I can't believe it!"

Patty flew higher into the tree, whose crown held the last rays of sun, while Sammy chased Becky around its trunk.

"How's it possible?"

"Helen don't hate me as much, I guess. Besides, she's tired of the constant howling."

"This is too wonderful," she squealed, intercepting and then tackling her sheepdog. "Sammy! You're going to have a brother!"

Shortly later, as Jerry and Claire pulled around to the back of the widow's house in the green coup wagon, Moon Doggy began to howl and Sammy wailed a response. The sheepdog bolted from the backseat door held open for him, skidding onto the packed dirt lot. "You'll hurt yourself," Claire chided the frantic dog, whose legs could not keep pace with his zeal.

The widow suddenly appeared above them on the porch. "That's the racket I'm talking about," she scolded, her long pointy face puckered sourly. Yet it instantly sweetened as she held up a dog leash. "Found it!" she announced, with a childlike grin. "Knew I had one; just didn't know where." Her small eyes gleamed.

Man and girl exchanged sly grins over the slight woman standing above, wearing a faded bib apron over a cotton dress. Though nearly summer, she still wore thick, woolen socks and loafers. Helen Whiner was a strange bird, which oddly enough made her likeable.

Claire bounded away, toward the wooded hillside and the barking dogs, while Jerry approached the bowing treads of the dry-rotting porch stairs. He looked up to the widow, nodding with respect. "Thanks, Helen," he said, lifting a foot to the first rise. He looked briefly down and then up again. "I'm not sure I've expressed my gratitude." He stopped for a deep breath, which she quickly filled with prattle.

"I got dog food here on the kitchen table," she said, spinning toward the ratty screen door that in an instant slammed behind her. Jerry hesitated, not certain whether to stay or follow, but before he could decide, she was back, hoisting a twenty-pound bag. He bounded up the stairs to relieve her of the burden.

"I love that dog, Helen," he said, grasping the bag. "Mike and me spent many an afternoon with him."

"You don't need to remind me," said the widow, suddenly angry. "You spent too much time goofing off together." She quickly turned, baffling him with her sudden change in temperament. He couldn't let her escape and so dodged between her and the screen door. "Listen, Helen. I need to show my appreciation. What if I fix these porch steps for you?"

Her scanty eyebrows jumped in surprise. "If it makes you happy," she said in her terse way. "Now get out of my way!" Jerry obliged, thereafter whistling happily as he loaded the dog food into the back of the wagon. Toward this musical call sprung two jubilant dogs, scaling the hillside from the barn. He turned to see flopping ears and wagging tails barreling toward him. The old man braced himself for the heft hidden beneath flounces of sheepdog fur. Sammy slammed into his thigh, while Moon Doggy sped in tight circles, stopping to howl into the air. Jerry laughed, slapping his knees.

"Come here, Moon Doggy," he said, grabbing the beagle up into his arms and shooting a look toward the kitchen window. The light above the sink was now on and he could see the widow smile, which completely surprised him. He smiled in return, holding the struggling dog tighter to his chest. In the dim light of dusk, deepened by surrounding trees, Claire opened the backseat door just as a four-wheeler hurtled into the clearing. Jerry urged Sammy into the back and then quickly toppled the beagle onto the crowded bench seat beside him. "Get in front," he ordered Claire, slamming the back door.

Billy bounced off his vehicle and charged toward them. With fingers he combed hair over his glass eye. "Hey, where're you taking Schooner?" he whined like a child, though he stood tall as a man.

"Your aunt will explain, Billy, but we're taking him with us," said Jerry.

"He's my dog!" Billy scrambled over to the passenger side of the car, where Claire sat with her door open. "You can't take him!" he shouted before grabbing the backdoor handle, but it was locked. He kicked the door.

"Hold on right there, mister," Jerry said, hurrying behind the car as Helen pushed through the screen door above. "Your aunt gave the beagle to *me*—not to Claire." Confounded, Billy looked upward to his aunt, now leaning over the porch railing, back lit in the yellow light of the kitchen. "What's he talking about?"

"Just this, Billy James Hollow," said Helen, "Schooner never was *your* dog and you don't care two cents about him. So stop your hissy fit." She spun around and marched back into the kitchen.

What happened next perplexed both Billy and Jerry. Despite the explosive situation, Claire popped from her front seat to strike a casual posture by the car, elbow propped atop its roof. Incredibly, she began chatting *at* Billy, for he was in no way participating. Annoyed by the distraction, he charged the opposite door, but Jerry stepped in front of it. Moon Doggy barked aggressively at his would-be captor. "Quit it!" Jerry ordered. The teen stepped back, chest heaving with emotion. "You can see him any time you want," the elder said less sternly. "Just come to the store."

Coasting toward them, Claire persisted in a careless attitude bewildering to both males. She couldn't lose this opportunity to tell Billy about Crawley's return. But if he wouldn't listen, then she'd announce it to Jerry, in hopes that the belligerent would finally pay attention. Following Jerry to the front seat, she said much too loudly, "Did you know that Robert Crawley is coming to stay at his lodge in the woods?"

"Yep, I know it." Jerry sat heavily into the front seat and started the ignition. "In fact, I got to mow the grounds there Sunday afternoon."

Claire, who had bended down to talk into the car, bolted upright. "What?"

Billy drew suddenly near. "I want to know, too."

Jerry shut off the ignition, sighing in resignation. "Okay, then. What exactly do you nosey bodies need to know?"

Claire led the investigation, conscious to include any question for which Billy would need an answer. He stood alongside her, soaking in every detail. Jerry explained that the caretaker, an old friend, had been hospitalized for two weeks and might now be placed in a nursing home. His daughter had called asking if he'd be willing, just once, to mow the grounds before the owner's arrival. Sammy wedged his big head between the front seats, slobbering all over the old man's arm with his panting tongue.

"Wait," said Jerry, looking anew at the boy, sifting ideas through his squinting eyes. "You know how to operate a riding mower?"

Billy snorted. "Of course."

"Share the mowing with me on Sunday. I'll pay you. My back won't take the strain." Billy hesitated. He stroked the hair over his glass eye, while his left grew with panic. "Wouldn't you like to see a billionaire's chateau?" Jerry urged, trying to entice the boy, who stared at him stupidly. "You've never been there, right?" he asked innocently.

The question put Billy on the defensive. "No!" he shouted.

"Then it's settled." Jerry started the ignition. "I'll call this evening to arrange things with your Aunt Lizzie."

7

Into the Sky

Saturday morning, Claire trod briskly through the woods, eager to see Ku-Khain and her family. For a month the female hawk and her mate Hakanyi had been tending their three chicks, feeding and vigorously protecting them. Whenever possible, Claire snuck away to the outcrop despite her mother's prohibition against doing so. Nothing could prevent Claire from checking on the safety of Ku-Khain—especially not now with Clyde Hollow on the loose.

She moved swiftly over a soft mat of soggy, decaying leaves. An overnight storm soaked the ground and sweetened the air filled with the pulse of trees shedding their raindrops. Claire heard but could not listen to the birds everywhere swelling with trills, whistles, and rapid chatter.

Instead her mind sank through a sea of worries and anchored in the chateau—Hollow's hideout—where she, Jerry, and Billy were to go the next day. Billy had little more than 24 hours to get word to his father. Would Clyde flee before their arrival or stay hidden, watching from the shadows? Surely he would never confront them. Would he? Try as she might, she couldn't dislodge a mental image of Hollow, drunk and delirious, aiming a rifle at her.

Something the width of a gun barrel prodded Claire between the shoulder blades. Blood flashed like a fuse through her body. A strangled breath squealed through her lungs. She twisted around to see her assailant—a sturdy, blunt-edged branch into which she had backed. Sinking with relief onto her knees, she suddenly understood. The situation was simply too dangerous to honor her promise to Victor. When home again, she would tell her mother and Jerry about Clyde hiding out in the chateau.

The decision liberated her. Tension flowed from her eyes and brow, carrying the debris of Clyde's image from her mind. Standing, she noticed sun-filled raindrops beaded on the leaves above her and heard a Carolina Wren chipping in alarm. The bird disappeared into the cavity of a dying walnut tree that held its nest.

"Hi Carolina," she said, stroking an image of this wren appliquéd on her tee shirt. She looked around for Sammy and Moon Doggy. Both dogs knew the way to the outcrop and took turns in a tongue-panting relay race, scouting ahead and then racing back to her. Neither was now in sight, but she didn't worry. She felt too relieved to worry.

Pushing through the wet mountain laurel, Claire scanned the faded blue sky for Hakanyi. Perhaps he would be away from the nest, scouting his territory for aggressors. She fervently hoped so because otherwise he might still attack her. She had hidden from his dive-bombing attacks throughout the early spring huddled under Jerry's wool-lined and hooded canvas coat. Such bulky armor was difficult to cart along on her outings (not to mention sneaking unseen from the house). But at last Hakanyi had relented—and not a day too soon—she could never have carried that heavy coat through May.

Preoccupied, she didn't notice a different threat, one whose long, cool body extended beneath the rock shelf onto which she stepped. The timber rattler cared only for what he could eat and so ignored the girl climbing atop the outcrop. His fare was chipmunk or mole, egg or hatchling, any warm-blooded (or not) creature that could fit through the portal of his unhinged jaw. Such prey was plentiful, despite the hawks that nested in the neighboring outcrop. The snake knew better than to approach their stronghold. Only once had he tangled with the nesting pair, nearly to become *their* food. The hawks had tried to carry him off but unable to bear his weight dropped him earthward, where he fell upon a huge cushion of debris. In need of heat, the snake slid from his damp hiding place toward a circle of sun within the mountain laurel.

Claire crossed the Fist, stopping three feet from its northern edge, which faced the adjacent outcrop called the Finger. She approached the ledge with proper respect, having before nearly fallen over its brink. Across the breach separating the two outcrops could be seen the nest, a large, sturdy construction built within an alcove of the cliff. Three nestlings were already standing erect, stretching and flapping their wings on the nest rim, eager to learn of the world beyond. In three short weeks they had transformed from white puffs of down with oversized eyes to proud would-be fledglings with broadening chests and strengthening legs. In two weeks more they'd leave the nest. For now, they hungrily awaited some meal, though neither parent was in sight. Ku-Khain, however, would not stray far from her chicks and so the girl waited.

Moments later, a hunting scream alerted all to Ku-Khain's approach. The fledglings whistled a chorus of shrill notes, clambering for position on the nest rim. Claire spun around to see the hawk flying in from the south, dropping altitude. Something struggled in the grip of her talons. Binoculars revealed a squirrel, not yet impaled, cradled in a deadly crib of talons. Lifting her face toward the fast-descending raptor, she took one step back and froze, conscious of the ledge. Beneath the raptor's steep descent she ducked as a tornado of gray fur dropped through the air and hit the rock face. A spasm of fur at her feet and Claire jumped back, grabbing her breath.

The ledge!

Yet the roiling fur advanced over the rock face and her every impulse screamed to retreat. Instead she leaped over the tortured body of the broken squirrel, whose tail whipped violently and then was still.

She stood over it, breathing hard. Was it dead? Dearly she hoped so for no one should bear such suffering. She touched her toe to its back, with no reaction. Prodding the limp body, she felt no resistance and knew it to be lifeless.

The hawk flew on to the nest, where hungry chicks demanded a meal. Their harsh cries of complaint drew Claire's eyes as Ku-Khain launched into the narrow inlet of sky, heading back to retrieve her fallen prey. What the raptor wanted lay dead at Claire's feet, yet the girl couldn't move, somehow snared inside the event. She felt herself rise and dip on the majestic wings plying toward her through the sky. The bobbing rhythm of the hawk's breast, its crimson cross a focus, hypnotized her. Closer and closer, larger and larger, the hawk grew, magnified as within a birding scope—but no! This was real space, real time. With Ku-Khain nearly upon her, Claire ducked and scooped the dead squirrel from the rock to fling upward and into the grasping talons of the raptor—girl and hawk united.

In the giving and taking, the two exchanged energy. Within her own human hands, Claire felt the power of the hawk's grip, and as Ku-Khain pulled upward, the girl felt herself lifting into the sky. She became hawk and her spirit soared. Higher and higher Claire rose until even Ku-Khain flew far below. Her rapid ascent, at first exhilarating, became terrifying, for the world might shrink into nothingness beneath her hawk-eyes. A breath froze in her lungs and a word boomed in her ear: *Hurry!*

Instantly the hawk spirit severed from her own and Claire slipped earthward, toppling into her body, crumpled onto the rock. For many minutes she lay as a heap of flesh and bone, shaken by the experience. In dreams she often soared high above the Earth. Was this then a dream? Pushing against the rock to sit upright, she felt weak and disoriented. Somehow, collapsing unconscious to the ground, she must have been swept into a brief dream, wherein a disembodied woman's voice—one she recognized but could not identify—shouted into her ear. It was the only explanation.

Shaking, Claire walked feebly from the outcrop. She scanned the trees beyond the mountain laurel, searching for Sammy. He was easy to spot among the low-growing shrubbery, a sprightly-stepping black and white hulk, weaving toward her through the tangle of greenery.

"Sammy!" she sighed with relief, wading through the wet maze to greet him. "You're such a dependable boy." She had completely forgotten about the beagle, who pushed past from behind, lifting his angel face to her reaching hand. "Moon Doggy!" The dog stared at her devotedly, everything sweet brimming from his soulful brown eyes. She kissed him heartedly on his smooth, white forehead. " Let's go home."

Both dogs eagerly, though somewhat clumsily, executed an "about face" on the footpath threading the woody shrubs. In single file, they squeezed through the wet laurel past an opening wherein lay the timber rattler, soaking up the sun.

Later that day, Victor headed toward the ringing phone with a bowl of cereal. His mother Rose was working the supper shift at the restaurant. Too hungry to wait, he shoveled the first spoonful of crunchy flakes into his mouth before answering the fourth ring with a garbled, "Hello."

Claire got to the point immediately. "Victor, I'm going to tell; it's too dangerous."

The mush sliding down his throat heaved upward within a gasp and he began to choke. Through the receiver, Claire could hear something crash and then spasms of strangled coughing. Terrified, she screamed, "Get your mother!" Seconds past while his throttled breaths, horrifying to hear, continued.

She pleaded helplessly into the phone. "Hang up, Victor! Can you hear me? Hang up! I'll call an ambulance." But he did not disconnect and she could not get a dial tone. In this dreadful moment she hated her mother for not having a cell phone. In utter misery she began to wail.

Louise bolted into the living room from the store through the swinging door. "What is it?" she cried, rushing to her distraught daughter. "What's wrong?" She grabbed the receiver from Claire's limp grasp and said, "Hello? Hello? Is anyone there?"

Now Jerry stood huddled behind Louise, looking to the girl, draped over the steps of the stairwell, sobbing into folded arms. "Yes, Victor, it's Claire's mother," Louise said, and the girl sprang like a cobra to snatch the receiver from her mother's grasp.

"Victor!" she screamed. "I'm sorry!" Now she stood, motioning the adults away, speaking only to explain her hysterics and thus dismiss them. "He was choking. I thought he might die."

Wearing expressions of relief and reprimand, Louise turned to head back into the store. "We'll talk about this later," she said. Jerry popped his wiry brows as if to say, "Looks like somebody's in trouble," and winking, turned to follow. With the swinging door fluttering behind them, Claire again spoke to Victor. "I was so scared. Are you all right?"

Victor knew he suddenly possessed leverage. "I almost choked to death," he said. "You sprang that on me just as I was swallowing." Claire apologized again, feeling guilty and therefore susceptible to Victor's wishes, chief being that she not break her promise and tell. However, when she finally explained the upcoming mowing expedition, he too felt anxious.

"So he's taking Billy?" Victor said, lifting large chards of glass from a lagoon of milk and flakes on the linoleum floor. He dropped these into the wastebasket dragged from beneath the kitchen sink. "I'm not sure if that's good or bad."

Having had more time to consider the implications, Claire offered an analysis. "I think it's good because I can go along to watch for his reactions." She moved to sit within the winding stairwell, lowering her voice to a whisper. "If Clyde is still hiding out, Billy will give him away."

The covert situation appealed to Victor. "Well, then I'll come, too, as a spy— "

Chapter 7

"You will?" Claire jumped upward. "Really! I swear I won't tell anyone."

"If Billy's still trying to hide his father at the chateau, it will be from you and Jerry. I'll be almost invisible."

Together they worked out the details, where Victor would station himself, how and when they would communicate and, most importantly, what they would do in case of an emergency—if Clyde should attempt anything dangerous. With plans in place, they awaited the coming day more excited than scared.

8

Spies and Schemes

Sunday, around noon, Victor sat beneath a purple cloud of fragrant petals buzzing with bees. Against his own heartbeat he had raced to get up the maple tree, over the wall, and beneath this rhododendron beside the chateau. So where were they? Unlike Claire, Victor did not fear Clyde, but he wondered if she was right. Did he insist on keeping the whereabouts of Billy's father secret simply to protect the Mars mission? He pulled a water canteen from his backpack and took a long drink.

He thought about the Red Planet and his gaming avatar, RedWing. For nearly a year, he had identified solely with his animated character, occupying a virtual 3-D universe. He entered that universe in mind and spirit—even in virtual body—each time he logged in. It was *not* a game, but another dimension, one wherein he could travel millions of miles through star-studded space toward a new world.

Yet with the mission about to resume, Victor now found himself preoccupied with his Cochiti name and identity: *Muh'nah'kain Kuhaia*, Black Bear. His father still called him "Little Bear," but he didn't share this detail with Claire. Yet it bothered him that when alone, she did not willingly use his native name. Time and again he called her Moon Woman, *Tahwach K'uyaw*, but she simply blushed, never returning the intimacy. Standing to stretch, he listened over the droning hum of bees for any sound of their entry through the high iron gate. Nothing. What was taking so long?

From his front jeans pocket he pulled a small suede pouch decorated on the flap with a circle of blue, red, and white beads. A fringe of red beads trimmed the bottom. Within was cornmeal used to feed his grandmother and grandfather spirits during prayer. His father had taught him a sacred Cochiti prayer in their Keres language but he felt too anxious to offer it. Instead, he pinched a portion of the silky, white powder, sprinkled it into the air, and uttered, "Thank you dear Creator, for everything is right in the world and nothing is wrong."

Then he sat again to wait.

Almost immediately he heard a commotion at the gate and so crept beneath the long row of rhododendron to the front corner of the chateau. The entrance gate stood several hundred feet away, at the end of a long, sinuous drive. Like Claire, Victor wore about his neck a light pair of birding binoculars, a present from his father. Through these he watched in total surprise as a stranger, a tall young man, pushed open one side and then the other of the high black iron gate.

Victor lowered the binoculars, lost in thought. Who was this stranger? Where was Claire? A girl's shrill cry jolted his heart and he found himself standing beyond the building. It was as if somehow he jumped in time and space from the corner to several feet beyond, in plain view under a hot sun. Another shriek pierced the air. He crouched to sprint, laser-like focus locked to the sound's source. And then he saw her—*them*—across a shrub and rock garden, Claire and another man, not the tall one of the gate but a much shorter man. His fast, bouncing step seemed boy-like, especially with Claire skipping alongside. They were both laughing.

Victor crouched lower, fingertips anchoring into the chocolate-colored mulch, newly spread for the season. It flowed everywhere, embracing islands of cultivated shrubbery. He scuttled backwards, slipping on the woodchips, toward the shelter of the chateau wall. At its corner, he dropped to hands and knees. From there he watched Claire and the shorter man walking from the gate and over a river of grey cobblestones, the gateway drive. It flowed like a river from a swirling mosaic of granite that formed a courtyard plaza dominated by a gargantuan marble fountain.

To see better, Victor crept to a nearby holly bush, wide and high. He could stand there, straight and tall, to peer with binoculars through a gap in the branches. The man and Claire were halfway between gate and courtyard, a couple hundred feet away, too far to hear what they were saying. He looked at the man and instantly knew: Robert Crawley. The smiling face belonged to the man in Claire's newspaper article.

Crawley wore dark locks in the perfect tousle of expensively styled hair. It fell in shaggy waves from a side part, dipping over a high brow in lose, spiral curls. His wide grin displayed perfect teeth, bright white, set in a strong jaw.

And his deep-set eyes, seen through binoculars, were shockingly blue.

Victor didn't like him.

He switched focus to Claire. An elastic grin, stretched to the utmost, burned with embarrassed pleasure. She stole glances toward the man, as if he were the sun, nodding heartily to his every assertion. Something Crawley said extracted such a squeal from her as was painful to hear. He lowered the binoculars, feeling foolish. Those earlier cries had not been of distress but unrestrained glee.

Victor faded back toward the building. The situation bothered him. Nothing was as they had planned. And where were Jerry and Billy?

As Claire and Crawley reached the mosaic plaza, a compact SUV entered the drive. Never had Victor seen anything so flamboyant. Custom painted in electric colors of green, blue, orange, and yellow, the design suggested some kind of tropical bird, most likely a parrot. The vehicle followed the drive wrapping around the courtyard. Almost too late did he realize—it headed directly toward him! Victor shrank quickly back behind the rhododendron and watched, with suspended breath, as the vehicle pulled to park at the building's edge. A dozen feet from where he crouched, someone stepped from the vehicle, the tall man from the gate.

As the man passed, Victor crept farther back along the wall, unsure what next to do. Being a spy was more complicated than he imagined. Should he wait beneath the balcony? If Claire got inside the house, maybe she'd think to call down information to him. Or should he wait near the back of the chateau, hoping to overhear conversations on the patio? Of Clyde Hollow and his possible whereabouts, Victor forgot completely. He took another swig of water and slid against the wall to think.

On the other side of the chateau, Claire followed Robert and his personal assistant, Glenn Weiler, along a cobblestone path to the upper terrace patio. They entered a low, yellow brick wall through a white iron gate. Claire couldn't believe how goofy she'd been acting since Jerry, Billy, and she encountered the men just outside the walled estate. Introductions had ensued after which Jerry and Billy went to fetch the mower while she accompanied Robert to the chateau. No doubt he thought her a silly girl. Cheeks burning hot and bright, she kept her glance downward, painfully conscious of her tinted lenses.

"Let's have some ice tea," said Robert, clasping his hands loudly, as though announcing a great idea, and Glenn headed reliably toward the kitchen. Claire had hardly noticed Glenn but for his unusual height, easily six foot, six inches. Otherwise she saw him only in contrast to Robert, whose presence electrified her.

Robert motioned her to join him at a white wrought iron table overlooking the terrace below. "We'll wait for your friends here," he said grinning, blue eyes sparkling beneath his low, dark brows.   Obediently she darted from behind her momentary refuge, a planter of tall exotic grasses.

The ornithologist slouched in his seat a bit to prop feet, fitted with gray and white running shoes, onto the wall of the terrace. "You've got a Rufous Hummingbird on your tee shirt," he observed.

"I like birds," she said shyly.

"Of course, the Rufous is a Western bird," he continued, "seen only occasionally here in the East—"

"Oh, I forgot!" she cried, cupping hand to mouth. Robert paused, perplexed by the girl's apologetic outburst. "It's a fall or winter visitor," she somewhat whined, more to herself than to him.

Robert clasped hands behind his head. "So you know a little something about birds?"

"Yes," she mumbled, still distressed at having worn the image of a western species. She only ever wore images of birds that reasonably might be seen in a given season or habitat. To do otherwise would ensure failure. And failure might weaken—even break—the enchantment that kept the birds coming to her.

Robert swung his feet from the wall and leaned into the table. "Do you always wear binoculars?"

She nodded. "But they're light, so I don't notice."

Amused but doubtful, he studied her expression. "Okay, then, tell me what you see." He waved her upward, to stand with him looking out over the garden. Claire had taken an inventory of these birds on her visit with Victor, so she showed no hesitation. "Well, lots of Ruby-throats," she began.

"Right."

"I hear a Baltimore Oriole, though I haven't spotted him yet."

"Good," he said. "They like the top of trees."

"Oh, there's a Indigo Bunting." She pointed to what appeared as a small blue fixture atop a pink dogwood bract.

"You're beginning to impress me," he said, folding arms across his chest. "What else?"

"There! That was a Song Sparrow singing . . . and another." She swept the binoculars to the terrace below, which held the marble sculpture of a Red-tailed Hawk. "Oh!" she said, realizing her opportunity. Now she could ask if the hawk was Big Red—her Ku-Khain. "I see a Red-tailed Hawk," she said shrewdly, smiling at him.

"Isn't she a beauty?" gushed Robert. "I had a New York sculptor do it for me almost ten years ago. Let's go down; you can see it up close." In her eagerness, Claire knocked over her chair and bent to pick it up. "I don't believe it," Robert said, his voice a dull monotone.

"I'm a klutz—" she said, lifting her face and then stopped, stunned into silence.

Before her upturned face hovered a Rufous Hummingbird, filling her ears with the drone of his wings. She dared not move for risk of chasing him away. The tiny male bird watched her, his iridescent red-orange throat flashing on and off as he considered her from different angles.

"You shouldn't be here, little fellow," Robert said, in a quiet, soothing voice. "How'd you get so lost?" In answer, the hummingbird flew a tight circle around Claire as she slowly stood, and then again hovered before her face.

"Hey! Anyone home?" A call from the side yard and the moment popped like a balloon. Claire knew the voice: Victor. The Rufous Hummingbird dipped in the air, a departing gesture it seemed, before soaring off into the garden. Acting host to the unexpected arrival, Robert didn't see the surprise or irritation in Claire's expression. He headed toward the gate to admit the newcomer.

Rocking onto his toes, scanning the patio, Victor pretended to be newly arrived and in search of his friend, Billy. "Hey, Claire!" he exclaimed in mock surprise. "Didn't expect to find you here." Claire feigned a pleasant greeting, though her snapping gaze held an entirely different message: *What in the world are you doing?* His unplanned entrance was totally disorienting. Robert escorted Victor to the table, where the conspirators awkwardly jostled to take a seat, repeatedly locking and breaking eye contact.

"You two kids catch up," Robert said, turning away. "I'll check to see if that tea is ready." He hadn't taken but a few steps when Glenn, wearing a concerned expression, pushed onto the patio. For the first time, Claire and Victor could plainly see his aristocratic face, his sandy hair combed back from a high forehead in the trim cut of an academy schoolboy.

"Robert," he said, pausing with the gravity of a heavy announcement, "someone's been living in this house."

9

Hawk of Many Names

Glenn might have called "fire" given the reactions of his young guests. Claire and Victor shot upward, but Robert saw only two startled kids. "Sit back down," he ordered. The agitated company obeyed, sinking slowly into their seats. "Glenn will bring out your tea," he said, waving his assistant back into the kitchen, "and then he and I will check into this. I'm sure there's an explanation."

Claire and Victor spent agonizing moments poised at the edge of their iron seats, waiting to speak freely. Finally, Glenn delivered their tea and disappeared with Robert inside the chateau.

"We have to tell," Claire hissed.

"They already know," insisted Victor. "Just not *who*."

"But we do!"

And so their argument again ignited, burning more brightly in Claire, fueled by her growing infatuation for Crawley. Against her sudden ferocity, Victor hadn't a chance, and he knew it. "Fine," he said, passion draining from his face. "Tell them." He stared at her stonily.

His unexpected concession made Claire uncomfortable. She blinked nervously, finding the straw with her lips. She took a deep sip. "Really?"

"I don't care," he said, standing. "But I won't be here when you tell them."

"You can't leave!" She erupted from the chair. "I don't want to tell them alone."

The sound of a riding mower filled the air. "You won't be alone," he said, turning away. "Jerry and Billy are here."

Confronted with the responsibility, Claire's will quickly faded and she agreed to withhold the information at least for a time. Smiling with relief and renewed affection, Victor sank back into his seat. "Thanks, Tahwach."

As the mower's engine grew louder, the two confidants anticipated events to come. What would Billy do when learning his father's hideout had been discovered? Claire firmly expected Jerry to connect Clyde Hollow to the break-in.

Below, engulfed in waves of deep, riotous grass, Jerry shut off the engine and climbed down from a shiny limousine of a mower, which Billy eagerly scaled to occupy the vacated seat. "Not now, Billy," said the old man, cupping a hand over his eyes against the sun. He looked up to the terrace wall, where the smiling conspirators frantically waved. "Hey, how did Victor get here?" he said, waving back.

Billy shot one look toward them and jumped from the seating platform, hitting the ground hard. He led Jerry over the upward sloping grounds and through the patio gate, just as Robert and Glenn spilled from the back entrance.

And so it began.

Chapter 9

To Victor and Claire, the next hour unfolded like the script of a play, a mystery, wherein only they (and Billy) knew "whodunit"—but could not say. When Robert Crawley announced the news of the chateau break-in, Billy's long jaw dropped, but the adults didn't notice. Robert shuttled Jerry inside to see the evidence, while Glenn stopped a stampede for the door.

"We want to see, too!" Claire howled.

Glenn gently smiled, crossing his arms in finality. Insulted and indignant, the three adolescents broke rank. Billy faded back as Claire and Victor returned to the table for their tea. Glenn disappeared from his post for an instant to return with yet another tall glass for Billy. "Sit with your friends," he said, guiding the boy toward the table. "I'll check back in a bit."

Billy sat obediently, situated between the other two. Claire and Victor bounced glances off him to each other. Then Claire suddenly stood, scooting free from the table and the boys. Spilling down the central staircase to the lower patio, she circled the magnificent marble statue of the Red-tail settling onto a tree limb. Was this her Ku-Khain? The hawk's empty white eyes held no answer.

With drifting thoughts she floated down the curving stone staircase into the cool, soothing sound of falling water. In the sun-drenched pool, orange-gilded koi shimmered, swimming lazily. A dozen birds cut the thick, heavy air with their cool crystalline melodies. Here, below the chateau, all was tranquil and beautiful. Here, without distraction, she could think. And here, quite belatedly, her mind opened to the most unsettling of ideas:

Billy knew where Ku-Khain nested.

Billy kept contact with his fugitive father.

Billy could—*would*—tell his drunken father where to find the hawk and her nestlings!

Why hadn't she thought of this before? Twisting round, scrambling to climb, she fell against the stone steps. Heedless of a scraped and bleeding shin, she took the steps two at a time. Reaching the top, she hurtled toward the marble sculpture, face upturned toward the boys who both wore surprised expressions. She noted this an instant before colliding into Robert Crawley. Bouncing backward, she might have toppled if not for Robert grabbing her wrist. Embarrassed, she asked urgently, "Are the police coming?"

"No police," he said pleasantly yet with the emphasis of a shutting door.

"Oh." Claire didn't understand. Hadn't Jerry told him about Clyde Hollow? Should she? Above, the boys had stopped snickering. Draped over the terrace wall, they listened intently to the exchange, which Robert redirected to the marble statue of the hawk.

"Meet my Alexandra!" He swept a hand upward toward the hawk's head. "She and I were once good friends."

"Who's Alexandra?" shouted Billy from above.

Billy's intrusion irritated Claire but Robert smiled more

broadly. "Let's invite the balcony audience to join us," he said. "Come on down!"

Billy pushed Victor for moving too slowly. "Hurry up," he cried, bounding past to fly down the stone steps, a hand held over his right eye. Victor followed at a leisurely pace down the staircase flanking the fountain and into the garden. Crawley, Claire, and Billy proceeded off to the right toward a semi-circular wall of tall cedar trees, trimmed into oblong spears. As the trio disappeared behind this wall, Victor stepped more sprightly through the unruly grass. On the other side, he found Claire and Billy seated together on a cast stone bench that followed the curvature of the tree line. Robert stood before them.

"Sit down, sit down," he urged, excitedly. "I'm about to tell a great story." Victor squeezed into a small space between Billy and Claire despite an expanse of seating on the high-backed bench. Neither occupant acknowledged his arrival other than to shift in their seats.

"Okay!" Robert clapped his hands. "Do I have your attention?"

Noting Claire's rapt expression, Victor wondered why Crawley bothered to ask. But of course he knew: the billionaire had an ego the size of his goofy grin. Claire, however, saw nothing goofy in the boyish man, whose eyes sparkled in the sun like mixed chards of sapphire and sky-blue glass. "I want to tell you the story behind my statue. You see, it's not the likeness of just any Red-tail." Robert paused for emphasis. "It's the likeness of Lexi, once my partner in falconry."

A meager sprout of respect pushed through Victor's dislike. "You're a falconer?"

"*Was* a falconer . . . a long time ago."

For the first time, Victor saw something genuine in the billionaire. And Claire saw someone just like herself, someone who understood what it meant to bond with a hawk, to soar in spirit with a fierce, free animal of the sky.

"I found her on the ground, too young to be out of the nest and so probably fallen from it. And since I knew a little something about birds," a coy smirk stressed the understatement, "I took her home." He looked up to the sky. "I trained her. It doesn't take long and you can't imagine the thrill—"

But Claire could imagine and wanted to say so. "When I was almost four a hawk found me!"

"Really?"

"I was lost in the woods," she gushed, "and Big Red— that's what the locals call her—pointed me out by screeching and circling the tree I was under."

Robert's dark brows jumped at mention of Big Red. He stepped toward her, brows settling again in thought. "You don't mean a hawk with a cross on her chest?"

"Yes!" Claire shouted, leaping to her feet. "I do!" A straight-arrow arm shot toward the terrace above. "That *is* a statue of Big Red, isn't it?"

Claire's excitement caught the man unprepared. "Yes. But I call her Alexandra." Claire spun toward Victor and stomped her foot, a gesture meant to carry an unspoken message only he could interpret: *I told you so!*

"So tell me," Robert nodded for her to settle again onto the bench, before which he crouched to better hear her story. Claire found his nearness distracting. She looked away from his deep eyes seeking her own shallow-lens forgery. During her tale telling, no one but Robert existed, not even Victor, who knew the story, though not as fully as now told. How on a warm spring day, she had napped with her mother on a picnic blanket in the woods. How she woke before her mother and wandered off, becoming lost.

"I wasn't afraid," she said, becoming more animated. "I remember picking little blue flowers and sitting under a big tree to stuff them into a rip in the seam of my teddy bear. The birds were singing and I remember waiting to hear a Barred Owl." She grinned. "Because that's the only bird call I knew. I remember looking up, hoping to see one in the tree—" Her eyes lifted in mimic, locking onto something above, so that everyone looked up.

"Oh, " she exhaled softly.

From the empty sky all eyes descended to land on her face.

"What do you see?" Robert asked, again surveying the sky.

Claire shook her head. "I saw a memory, one I didn't know I had." She looked to Victor. "It was a hawk, looking down at me from a limb in the tree. I think it was Ku—" she stopped, swallowed, and then bit her lower lip. "I think it was Big Red."

To Robert Crawley the idea of a newly captured memory was not as interesting as the tale at large and so he urged her to continue. However, to Billy the story of Claire and Big Red's history was wholly new. His experience of the local hawk had been through the distorted lens of his father's obsession to shoot and stuff it as a trophy. And as a youngster with a BB gun, he had been happy to shoot at anything, especially birds, which made great moving targets. But after losing his right eye to an accidental shooting, he lost all interest in guns and shooting, to the great dismay of his father.

While the others kept pace with Claire's narrative, Billy wandered mentally over the wreckage of a recent experience —the day his drunken father had held him, Victor, and Claire at gunpoint. At the first opportunity, Billy had snatched the rifle and thereafter found himself aiming it at the crimson cross on Big Red's chest. Yet he couldn't squeeze the trigger. Why? Was he a sissy, as his father claimed? His father had shoved him away and aimed, greedy for the kill. A single shot and the legendary hawk forever would be Clyde's trophy. Yet Billy rose from the floor with tidal force that knocked his father down, crippling his shot and his chance.

Only weeks in the past, the episode seemed a faded dream. Even so, it whispered something to him, something he couldn't quite hear but nonetheless felt, a connection to these people in his company, all—like him—with a tie to the hawk.

"Kids! Up here—NOW!"

Jerry's strident call from the upper terrace reached Claire and the boys below, hidden behind the ring of cedar trees. All jumped but Robert. He tidily unfolded from his crouched position before Claire to smooth the creases in his white shorts and stretch. "We'll finish another time," he said, standing back as they filed away, Claire last to leave. When she looked back, he winked. "I want to hear more about you and Big Red."

10

Claire Smells a Rat

Trudging over white gravel under a hot sun, Jerry bristled with indignation. "What a fool," he muttered, rocking his head. "Some billionaire!" he added, volume rising. Stopping abruptly, turning back, he waved a fist at the gleaming chateau and yelled: "Not a dime's worth of commonsense!" Claire and Billy converged before the distracted man, pressing him onward to the car. Neither knew why he was so angry but expected soon to find out.

Disgruntled, Jerry didn't notice Victor's abrupt departure nor think to ask how the boy had come to be at the chateau. Claire directed her elder into the oven-hot car through the door held open by Billy. "The gall of that man," Jerry said, slamming a thick palm against the hot steering wheel. He switched on the ignition and all urgently lowered their windows.

"What on earth happened?" Claire asked, angling toward Jerry in the front seat. Billy knelt on the rise of the back floor. His large dirty-nailed fingers clasped her headrest, and his horse face hung so close she could see patches of downy stubble on his chin and jaw.

"Sit back, Billy," she cried, smacking his hand. But he didn't flinch.

"I want to hear!"

Chapter 10

Jerry switched off the ignition and slid back his seat, hoisting sideways to see them both. He scratched and stroked his beard considering where to begin. Eyes and words screwed small, he began. "Crawley didn't call the police because—" he lifted a bushy brow and his voice boomed, "because he suspects the caretaker, my friend Ben."

"That's insane!" Claire bounced onto a boney knee and bumped her head on the ceiling. "Didn't you tell him about Clyde Hollow? He's the one who stayed there—I know."

Jerry threw a glance toward Billy, collapsing into the back seat in what looked like a state of shock. "You don't *know* anything of the kind, Claire," Jerry said. "Besides, I'm not interested in who's guilty, only who isn't—my friend Ben.

Claire felt Billy's panic and remained quiet as Jerry recounted Crawley's twisted rationale for suspecting his loyal employee of ten years. He cited the billionaire's theories, everything from senility (Ben was losing his mind) to necessity (maybe the plumbing failed in the care-keeper's cottage). Whatever the reason, Crawley insisted he speak first with Ben before calling in the police.

"I know what he's thinking." Jerry twisted back to his steering wheel to Claire's great relief because she was suddenly preoccupied with a severe need to use a bathroom. "He doesn't want people knowing his precious stone palace sits empty 50 out of 52 weeks a year." Again he started the ignition.

Claire couldn't listen because her entire attention centered on a swelling bladder. Sheepishly, she admitted to the situation. Jerry sighed loudly, now shutting off the ignition. He waved a hand toward the chateau. "I can't go back there," she cried, groping the door handle. "Let me go in the woods."

"Wait." He dug a set of keys from his front pocket. "You can use Ben's cottage."

Billy sprang to the edge of his seat and grabbed the keys extended to Claire. "I have to go, too."

Claire slammed her back against the seat, folding arms tightly across her chest. She stared sullenly out the windshield while the car crawled from the gravel lot to Ben's drive, a couple hundred feet down a wooded lane. But before the car could roll to a stop, Billy had a leg outside the door. "I go first," he yelled, pitching headlong from the vehicle.

"Some gentleman," Jerry muttered, though Claire appeared relieved to let him go without her.

Billy jogged down a dirt drive to the waiting cottage, a cozy hulk of stone squatting in a circle of sun. Like the chateau, the one-story house was built of limestone and roofed with orange clay tiles, an elegant cap to an otherwise modest abode. Claire smirked to see Billy twice drop the key in his urgency to enter.

Something in how Billy stealthily slipped through the door, closing it quickly behind, struck her as odd. And instantly she knew—Clyde Hollow hid, waiting, inside Ben's cottage.

Claire knew she must immediately intervene but didn't know how, other than to get out of the car. "I can't wait!" she blurted, pushing out the door to plunge down the short drive trimmed with ox-eye daisies. She jumped these, skidding to a halt in front of a glossy red door. Huffing with effort, she glanced over a shoulder to wave to Jerry over the pretty patch of wildflower pasture carved from the woods that was Ben's yard.

Before she could pound on the door, it flew open. Billy glanced beyond her to the car. "I'm done. Your turn." He moved to pass but she didn't step aside.

With heaving breath, she said, "I know he's in there."

Billy darted an anxious eye from her to Jerry. "You're nuts," he said, shoving by her. "Nobody's in there."

"Right. He's probably in the shed by now."

Billy froze. He turned slowly, face crumpled in consternation. Both knew they had only seconds.

"Victor and I won't tell—for now," she said, nodding to Jerry with a pleasant expression to conceal their exchange. "But then you can't tell, either."

"Tell what?" He stepped toward her, insistent.

For Jerry's benefit, she hollered, "I'll just be a minute," and nodded for Billy to lead her through the door. A rank smell of stale smoke insulted their lungs. Neither attended to the details of the pleasant interior, a common floor space but for the bathroom. They stepped behind the open door.

"Don't tell your father about Big Red—where she's nesting or anything." She searched his solitary eye for sincerity but found only fear. She grabbed his arm. "You haven't already?"

"No!" He pushed her hand away. "Stop grabbing me," he said and stomped out the door. Claire scooted across the living space, walls a perfect pale yellow, to a corner room with an open door.

"Poor Ben," she thought, ducking into the small bathroom, brilliant with afternoon sun from a window above the tub. Though not knowing him, she could imagine the old man's dismay on returning to find his fresh, tidy home defiled by Billy's foul father. Washing her hands afterward, she turned to look out the window. A garage twice the size of the cottage, painted barn red, stretched across the back. Somewhere inside Clyde hid like a rat. She shivered to think of it, looking down into the tub where grimy dirt ringed the shiny white porcelain. A wet cigarette butt smashed onto a corner ledge drooled a yellow-brown stain down the side. "Yucchhh!" she cried and darted from the room, rubbing wet hands against her shorts.

At home, Claire couldn't wait to report to Victor. She hurried with the phone receiver to hide behind the thick oak door of the twisting stairwell. This enclosed passage to the upstairs was one of many eccentric features in the 150-year-plus home. And she loved it like her own secret hideaway. Against two zealous canines, nails scuffing the floor in haste to join her, Claire shut the door. Yet with the beagle's first howl of protest, she relented. Otherwise, her mother or Jerry would investigate.

Sammy and Moon Doggy jostled for position beside Claire on the fanning twist of stairs. Where the steps were widest, the sheepdog sprawled behind her, his tail whipping her face, his fur smelling like dirty socks. On the narrow inside tread, the beagle groped for a foothold, slipping repeatedly and scraping her skin with his claws. From between this panting, slobbering pair, she bolted on a headlong rush up the stairs. The dogs clambered to follow but got shut outside the door of her sunken bedroom (its floor was one step lower than the rest of the upstairs). She belly-dived onto the bed and dialed Victor.

The exchange of information between friends was rapid and breathless. She told him of the group's encounter outside the gate with Robert Crawley. He told her of his endless suspense waiting beneath the rhododendron. They critiqued Crawley's car, Claire thinking it "unique" and Victor "weird." And while he didn't comment on her silly behavior toward the obnoxious billionaire, old enough to be her father, he did complain loudly that she told him of Big Red.

"So don't tell Crawley anything more about her," he said, voice bleeding.

Claire rolled onto her back, talking to the low ceiling. "He already knows her, Victor. They were even partners." Propping an ankle atop bended knee, voice swooning, she said, "Just imagine."

"Who cares?" he cried. "She's Ku-Khain now. *We* named her, remember?"

"Of course!"

"And I don't want him to know about her—or her chicks."

"Okay, okay," she said, dragging herself off the bed. "Stop being so cranky." She had yet to announce the biggest news, of her confrontation with Billy, news that would not make Victor happy. For moral support, she opened the door and the room sucked in the dogs like a force of nature. Sammy jumped onto the bed while the beagle strained at its side, whimpering to be pulled up. In this happy bedlam, she began her confession.

The entire time she talked, explaining and qualifying every word spoken to Billy, Victor said nothing. Even when she paused for him to speak, he still said nothing. When unable to bear his silence any longer, in her most convincing tone, she concluded: "Don't you see? This simplifies everything. Now we can keep tabs on Clyde through Billy." Air held in her lungs, Claire waited for a response.

"How could you be so stupid?" he shouted and disconnected. Victor's head throbbed. The blood pulsed in his temples and his eyes ached.

"That was terribly unkind," said his mother, pulling from the refrigerator iceberg lettuce to plop beside a tomato on the counter. The thin, ragged woman turned fretful eyes to her son. "Would you like someone to call you *stupid*?"

Chapter 10

"Someone should!" he said, pounding a fist beside the wall phone. He stomped from the small square kitchen, smelling of burnt coffee, through a squeezed living room to his cramped bedroom. If not for his father, coming to take him to the cabin, Victor would cry. Instead, he slammed the bedroom door.

How did things get so out of control? Too late he realized that Claire was right. Whatever made him think they could ignore something so huge as finding a fugitive and his hideout? Not just any fugitive but Billy's father and not just any hideout but a billionaire's woodland retreat. He grabbed a small duffel bag from beneath his single bed and slammed it onto the mattress.

11

Billy Wins a Confidant

During the drive to his father's cabin, Victor felt less agitated. The road rolled and twisted through the state forest and late day sunlight settled over the ground like a heavy, golden fog. Victor closed his eyes and pushed his face into the evening air. It smelled sweet and wet, similar to melon. He inhaled deeply and smiled. "Why can't I live with you, Dad?"

"You're living with me right now," George said, tugging Victor's wind-whipped hair. At times like this, Victor felt like he could tell his father anything. He even considered confessing about Clyde Hollow and the chateau. But that would require revealing a larger deception, which he wasn't prepared to do. And lying to his father was difficult. The man could sink his gaze, like a fishing line, into Victor's own and pluck out whatever he sought.

Coincidently his father turned the conversation to the chateau break-in. He had learned of it from Jerry, who called in a state of extreme agitation. And more, he learned that Ben Fellow, the billionaire's top suspect and a current hospital patient, had slipped into a diabetic coma.

"Jerry is upset," said George, slowing for a chipmunk scurrying over the road. "A life-long friend may be dying, and Ben can't defend himself against Robert's charges."

"Crawley's a jerk," Victor said, dropping an arm to dangle outside his window.

"Misguided, maybe."

Victor drummed fingers against the outside door, his pulse quickening. He tried to speak casually, as with a stray thought. "The police never caught Clyde Hollow." He glanced out the window. "Why isn't he a suspect?"

"I'm sure he is," George said.

"Really?" Victor couldn't disguise his pleasure and didn't try.

That evening George surprised Victor with all manner of fun activities outlawed by his mother. The man didn't delight in undermining his wife's authority but did so for Victor, who would otherwise wilt under her oppressive protection. Both desperately believed that with love and time, her mind and spirit would heal. But until then, father and son kept their indiscretions secret.

Under a full moon they swam in the dark, cold lake. Over the placid surface, the moon's brilliant disk spilled sparkling trails of light. Whichever way he swam, a luminous channel beckoned. Yet Victor stayed close to the shoreline with his father, laughing and talking in a hushed reverence for the night. Behind their voices, thousands of male crickets fiddled for mates while frogs sang solo performances in deep baritone or soprano.

Wet, their skin taut with cold, they changed quickly into dry clothes beside a dark fire ring. Inside the ring, an expertly constructed tent of wood waited. Kerosene and sulfur scenting the air, George lit the tinder, bringing to life a beautiful fire. On wool blankets they sat close to the fire's blaze. Cozy in its warmth, embraced by the light of its flames, father and son talked of their time apart.

Victor loved to listen—and watch—as his father talked. The gentle tilt of his head, hands that sculpted images from the air, voice a medicine to his heart, wearied by a high-strung mother. Of course, they talked about her; they always did. But they had given up trying to coerce her to seek professional help. She simply wouldn't. So they prayed for her, putting her care into the hands of the Creator, knowing that all would be well, eventually.

As the night wore on and the moon climbed higher, they talked less, staring contentedly into the fire. Victor's thoughts roamed to Claire and their recent conversation. He regretted his nasty remark, though their predicament was entirely her fault. Still, he felt guilty and needed to validate his anger. "Claire makes me mad sometimes," he began, pausing for his father to nudge him on.

George stood with a strong stick to poke the dying fire. "Why so?" A shower of embers lifted into the night sky.

"She acts like such a know-it-all." Victor pulled a knee to his chest. "Like I'm so dumb because I don't know this or that bird."

While patrolling the fire's edge, George considered his

son's complaint. "Does she call you dumb or do you just feel that way?"

Victor was looking for confirmation, not analysis, and so tried to drop the subject, but his father wouldn't. Together they then wandered the maze of his relationship with Claire, a route made even more complex for the passages keep hidden by Victor. They covered much ground, including Claire's special relationship with birds, particularly the Red-tailed Hawk known by his father and locals as Big Red.

"I think the Red-tailed Hawk is Claire's animal guide," George said. He sat cross-legged in a loose lotus position beside his son.

Victor lay on his stomach, chin propped on folded arms, staring into the glowing mound of charcoal. "You mean Big Red?" Victor would not divulge—not even to his father—the secret name he and Claire had given the raptor.

"I mean the *spirit* of the Red-tailed Hawk guides and protects her. Big Red is an expression of that spirit and is obviously tied to Claire. Look how many times they've touched one another's lives. And didn't Big Red lead me to her in the woods that day so many years ago?"

Victor smiled, proud as always of his father's part in discovering a toddler lost in the woods, yet learning only within the year that the girl had been Claire.

"As an animal guide, the hawk gives special vision, not only to see better but to see from a different perspective, as a hawk with an aerial view of the world."

Victor pushed himself up to sit on his knees. "Is that why Claire's eyes are different, because she has special sight?" George knew of Claire's unusual eye color from having rescued her as a honey-eyed child.

"Maybe so." George stood to pick up a metal pail. "Now let's get some water from the lake to put out this fire. It's time for bed. We've got to leave extra early if I'm to get you to school in time." Across the dark lake, somewhere in the forest beyond, arose a shrill, pulsing song.

"What's that?" Victor roused from his contemplation. Stepping briskly alongside his father, curiosity lighted his face.

"A Whip-poor-will, of course." His father mimicked the song of the nightjar by quickly repeating the phrase, *Whip poor Will.*" Victor joined his father, matching the frantic tempo of the bird's quivering song. Together they rattled their voices, loud and full, sending their song into the night.

While Victor sang into the night, Claire fought it. She tossed in bed on turbulent waves of moonlight, blowing over her in the breeze of a warm night. Victor's reproach bounced about in the chamber of her mind, driving her to exhaustion but not to sleep. *How could you be so stupid?*

After school the following day, Claire worked alone in the garden. Pulling weeds under a humid, gray sky suited her ill temperament. From the grove of cherry trees on the hillside above, an Eastern Towhee watched, grasshopper clasped in her bill. The bird called out in alarm—

Ter-weet! Ter-weet! Ter-weet!

Between rows of beets Claire stood, clumps of purslane dangling from her fist. "Oh, stop complaining," she grumbled, sinking onto her knees into the next row. The female Towhee however would not desist and again called out before diving from her perch to fly out over the garden above Claire—

Hur-ry! Hur-ry! Hur-ry!

Startled by this strange refrain, Claire strained her neck to follow the bird. Surely the towhee had not called the word *Hurry*, yet that's what she thought she heard. Squinting skyward, she gasped to see Billy's long, glum face blocking the sky. He stood directly above her.

"Billy!" she cried.

He bent farther over, the hair that covered his right eye hanging free of it. "Did you tell anyone?"

"Don't crowd me!" She pushed up as he stepped back, brushing dirt from her hands. "No!"

"Did Victor?" He pressed in again, like a dolt without manners.

"Of course not!" She stumbled backwards out of the garden. "What are you doing here?"

Billy nodded toward the house, hundreds of feet distant and much too far for Claire's comfort. "I told your mom I was here to see Schooner."

She marched toward the house but quickly turned. "Did you tell your father that we know?"

"No."

"And you haven't said anything about Big Red, right?"

Billy responded with a glower. Above them in the pasture, Sammy and Moon Doggy were investigating rabbit holes and other haunts of interest. For reasons no one but the dogs understood, the sheepdog no longer ran off—at least not in the company of the beagle. Somehow, Moon Doggy acted as a natural restraint to Sammy, who was now content to keep himself within their 17 acres (perhaps more since dogs don't know property lines).

On hearing Billy's voice, the sheepdog pulled a wet, quivering nose from deep within the hole of an often-harassed rabbit. Moon Doggy flipped off his back, from a deep bed of clover, to his short legs. Both cocked heads and lifted ears to confirm the sound. But while Sammy dashed toward the hillside, displacing dozens of white butterflies, Moon Doggy turned opposite to wade more deeply into high grass.

At an impasse in their exchange, girl and boy welcomed the distraction of a sheepdog plunging toward them through the grove of cherry trees. It was hard to manage a dour mood with so much joy charging their way. Billy tried nonetheless.

"Where's Schooner?" he demanded.

"*Moon Doggy,*" she corrected. "Still up on the pasture, I guess." Claire glanced to the hillside and saw a calamity of muscle and fur heading straight for her frail tomato plants.

"Stop him!" she shouted. Billy understood, cutting through the garden at a diagonal to intercept Sammy in a perfect collision of brawn and boy. Brawn won. Billy lay on his back, winded, knees awkwardly poking the air. Sammy leapt over his torso, positioning himself for access. He sought the boy's face with an eager tongue.

"Arrrgghhh!" Billy rolled from under the wet muzzle, and tried to sit up, driving the sheepdog to a frenzy of affection. Straining against the boy's outstretched arms, the dog sought the skin of his face and neck. Billy howled in gleeful protest as Claire finally reached them. Groping to stand in the deep grasses, he couldn't rid himself of the grin born of Sammy's wet, mushy muzzle and warm, tickling tongue.

Claire stared, amazed, at the transformation a smile made to Billy's face. Hollow cheeks rounding robustly changed the entire atmosphere of his countenance. Even the gloomy fog typically veiling his good eye seemed to evaporate. Without discussion, the two headed up the hillside, Sammy charging the summit in advance. A heavy mist thickening the late afternoon air clung to their skin. "Watch for animal holes," she said. "They're everywhere but you can't see for the tangles."

Billy grunted and they climbed without speaking. Reaching the top, looking across a large pasture under a low, steamy, gray sky, he finally spoke. "Why didn't you tell?"

Sammy pounced after something scurrying in the grass as a soft rain began to fall. "Victor didn't want to rat you out." She glanced down, hesitating. "Billy, aren't you afraid of your father?"

He bent to pick up a short, heavy stick and flung it far into the air over the pasture. "Nah." They both looked to see if Sammy would chase it, but the dog's nose was back in a rabbit hole. "He's just a drunk."

"Drunks do stupid things," she said, fighting an urge to push the limp hair from his eye. She didn't think of her own yellow-gold eyes, hidden behind tinted lenses.

He caught the flick of her gaze and patted the hair, oily from being endlessly stroked, into place. He felt exposed and tired. The truth of her words left him suddenly defenseless. Behind his glass eye, a video played of his father's bizarre behaviors, everything from abducting him from school to holding Victor and Claire at gunpoint. Under the weight of this emotional burden, he suddenly sagged. Claire pulled him toward an ancient pear tree, remnant of a long ago orchard. "Let's sit under here, out of the rain."

Slumping against the tree's cracked, black trunk, he hung his head in submission. He was so tired of hiding and fighting. He needed help. He needed to tell someone everything about his father's plans. So he told Claire.

She didn't dare interrupt Billy for fear he might abandon the telling altogether. Intently she listened, nodding sympathetically. Nor could she have looked away, fascinated by the expressions animating his face, no longer dull like a donkey or furious like a bull but filled with emotion. She watched his expressions until jolted by a final declaration—his father was leaving. Elated, she sprang from the ground, nearly knocking into the tree limb overhead. "When?" With his tortured exhalation, she sank back to the ground.

"Not till he has money for the trip."

At once she cried, "You can't steal for him!"

But that was not his intent. He would earn the money as a groundskeeper for Robert Crawley. Already the job was his, with payment on completion of discrete tasks. Thus mowing the grounds would earn him $100, while weeding the flowerbeds—all of them—would net $200. "The sooner I can get it done, the sooner dad will leave."

"When do we start?" piped Claire, standing again, this time more cautiously.

Billy looked at her stupidly. "Huh?"

12

A Cerulean Surprise

The following Saturday, Claire sketched a vague cover story for her mother, one that didn't include riding with Billy on the back of a four-wheeler over public roads and private property. The truth, if told, would certainly provoke a verdict of "dangerous and illegal." Besides, her sudden association with a recent enemy and older boy could only be viewed with suspicion.

Louise had expanded her one-room grocery to include a morning coffee shop, serving a mug of coffee and slice of pie for $3.00. Two additional tables were crammed into the long narrow storeroom to oblige these customers, mostly elders like Helen, who even now sat at the table by the door. And Jerry's pie-making duties expanded from once a week to every other day, something he didn't like. Neither did Claire, whose duties expanded from weed puller to busgirl to dishwasher.

With chores completed, she pedaled down the Kelly Store Road till out of sight. Hauling the bike into the woods, she dropped it beneath the skirt of a bushy spruce, and ran on to Helen's, where she was to meet Billy. Through a corridor of high ferns she followed the deer trail, a dark part in the green growth. Over skinny boles of fallen trees, she jumped like a runner over hurdles. Sunlight dripped through the tree canopy into radiant puddles on the woodland floor. Feet stuttering, she descended a winding shoulder of the ridge toward the creek spanned by a moss-covered, rotting trunk of a once-massive red oak. Groping her way across, she then scaled the wooded ridge toward the back of Helen's property. Billy waited for her on the steps of his aunt's back porch.

On Claire's approach, he popped from the top step and jumped to the ground. His hair floated in the air like a breezy curtain. Never had she seen it so clean and shiny. No oily slab lay plastered against his socket, only a fringe of hair loosely draping his glass eye. "You ready, Belle?" he said, strutting toward the four-wheeler, an old, no-frills machine, built low to the ground and splattered with dry mud. Lashed onto a metal grid behind the seat was a leather duffel bag.

She followed him. "Sure," she said, wondering at his use of her last name.

He handed her a battered half-face helmet, without a shield, and then put on his own, more complete unit. She struggled with the chinstrap, squinting at the sun squeezing through the tree cover. Billy straddled the seat, looking over his shoulder for her to mount behind him on the long leather bench, cracked and torn. She did clumsily, not certain what to do with her hands.

"Hold on," he instructed, switching on the ignition. The engine roared to life, snorting gas fumes. Only as they bolted forward did she grab the bars of a metal grid that wrapped around the seat. The first bump lifted her from the seat and then slapped her back down, just as he took a sharp corner. To keep from sliding off, she grabbed the metal rack opposite.

"Let me off!" she screamed, pounding on his shoulder, as they sped toward the end of Helen's lane. Billy gunned the engine, ignoring her protest, and ripped out onto the road. Too soon he took a skidding turn into a dirt lane. Claire shut her eyes, crouching against his back. Small pebbles sprayed the side of her face and she gagged on a cloud of dirt. Out of the turn, she punched hard between his shoulder blades.

"Hey!" he protested.

"I'll kill you!" she yelled through the noise.

He revved the engine to make her wince but then slowed to a coasting speed. He spoke over his shoulder. "This is a private lane. We'll follow it to a four-wheeler trail."

Watching the ground creep alongside, Claire considered jumping off. If so, now was the time. She released her white-fisted grip on the metal rack and imagined the dismount, but the impulse to jump didn't follow. Searching for resolve, she plunged the depth of her lungs with a deep inhalation. Still nothing. If anything, she felt less anxious and so slumped into resignation. In the shade of hemlock, pine, and oak trees, they crawled down a long, twisting dirt lane.

The ground rolling pleasantly beneath her, Claire's thoughts ambled into the near future. She imagined Robert Crawley's bright smile and dark, tousled curls, but mostly his disarming eyes—fissures of deep blue in a Caribbean sea.

Chapter 12

Hidden beneath her outer sweatshirt was the image of a Cerulean Warbler. She chose the sky-blue and white bird for its local rarity, to draw it to her while in his company. Robert would be so impressed, just as when the Rufous Hummingbird orbited her like a moon. But until with him, she would conceal the image; otherwise the warbler might arrive too early.

Without warning, Billy hit the throttle hard, accelerating quickly and throwing up the front end. Claire clutched his torso to keep from falling off. He felt slight, a young tree bending in the wind. The front tires slammed to the ground, expelling her breath. "What's wrong with you?" she screeched to the fiberglass helmet, more penetrable than his thick skull.

For the rest of trip, she crouched inward, intent on nothing but survival. Eyes closed, body tuned to movement, door to the mind shut. She felt the ground rise, fall, and spin beneath her; felt the air warm or cool upon her face; and behind closed lids saw light and shadow. Not until hearing gravel under wheel did she surface, like a swimmer pushing upward to gasp air. With weak legs she dismounted while the engine idled.

"I've got stuff to give my dad," he said, spinning the quad around. "Say I'm getting the mower." Wheels skidding, he drove away. Claire pulled off the helmet, stiff and unstable on her feet. Heart racing, she walked to the main gate. It was unlocked. She set the helmet on the ground against the limestone wall and stood to stare through the high iron bars. Above the chateau appeared a fairytale castle gleaming in the sun. She pushed open the gate to slip through.

Glenn met her at the small patio gate, his friendly smile a calming sedative. Untouched by worry lines, his open, earnest face carried a philosophy: take life in stride. And being a man of exceptional height, each stride was long and slow.

She followed him through French doors into the kitchen, a room of antique white cabinets and stone floor covered by cotton rugs. Afternoon light from the casement windows flooded the long rectangular room dominated by a stone-faced work island. Behind him she trailed past creamy ceramic tile countertops accented with rustic urns, copper pots, and hand-painted European pottery. From a stainless steel refrigerator embedded within a stone wall, he pulled a glass pitcher of iced tea.

"Is Mr. Crawley here today?" she asked shyly. Glenn poured her a tall drink, which she hastened to accept.

"Yes, but he's busy." He smiled kindly, setting the pitcher onto the island counter of oak. "Is Billy outside now?"

She took a deep drink of the cold, sweet tea. Nose buried in the glass, she muttered, "Getting the mower."

"Oh," he said, heading to the doors. "The garage is locked. Drink your tea. I'll be right back." The door clicked shut and her mind opened to the situation: she and Robert were alone together in the house.

Across the long room, opposite the kitchen appliances, an alcove held another limestone wall, this one with a fireplace and heavy beam mantle. To its front and side sat a rustic oak table and chairs padded with sunny yellow and poppy red cushions. A colorful bouquet of fresh flowers graced the table center. Toward this cheery alcove she drifted, musing over details of the room, until caught unexpectedly by an archway. To her left, it offered passage farther into the chateau.

She stood, sipping tea, staring into the archway. It did not lead directly into an adjacent room but softly angled to the right as a hallway. She poked her head into the entry, only to find that after several feet, the white stucco hall wound gently to the left. Against its curving wall shone light from the room into which it led. She crept inside for a quick peek.

Greeting her gaze at the other end was a spacious foyer. Stepping cautiously out onto its polished marble floor, she lifted her face upward to a vaulted ceiling with ribs of crystal ice. Or so it appeared. Skylights of textured glass banded the arched ceiling, filling it with the glow of sparkling sun. Claire took a deep breath and stepped farther out. The foyer ran from a side entrance door, about 20 feet to her right, to an elaborate French door, some 30 feet to her left. And behind its span of beveled glass could be seen the greenery of an interior courtyard.

Claire sighed with the opulence of her surroundings and glanced back to the security of the hallway behind her. In a count of three, she would decide whether to return or continue forward. Squeezing eyes shut, she spoke aloud, quietly, "One, two—"

"Three!" A man's deep voice pierced the stillness.

Claire opened her eyes. Directly across from the foyer, not a dozen feet away, stood Robert.

"What happens now?" he said, with a chuckle, leaning against a white column, one of two, marking the entry hall to the main entrance behind him. Arms folded at his chest, Robert's dark, wavy hair grazed the collar of his white Polo shirt. Against it his skin shone a deep sun-baked brown.

Claire felt the glass, wet with condensation, slipping through her fingers. Clutching it with both hands, she stared as if a bomb were about to explode.

"So you're a birder and a break-in artist," he said, stepping sprightly to relieve her of the burden. He took it from her tangled fingers, grinning with amusement. Mortified, she stared into his face.

"Glenn told me to wait—you see I was in the kitchen—" she stepped backward, frantic to explain. Her white-lashed eyes flashed. "He's the one who gave me the tea."

"Sounds good. I'll get one, too." He herded her toward the hallway and into the kitchen where he poured a glass of tea for himself and then led her to the patio. Outside, she felt less jittery but not much. They sat at the patio table overlooking the gardens, a quenching rustle of fountain water below.

"Binoculars again, I see." He leaned into the curving back of the wrought iron chair. "You always wear them, right?"

She nodded, tipping the glass so that its ice cubes banged against her teeth.

"But today you've no bird on your shirt."

She hiccupped, grabbing her mouth to keep the tea from spilling out. "Bathroom," she said through splayed fingers, thrusting upward to hurry toward the kitchen door.

"Back wall of the kitchen nook," he called after, pleasantly distracted by the adolescent's foibles. To the distant sound of the mower she returned wearing a different shirt, one stamped with the image of a blue and white Cerulean Warbler. "Better?" he said, sitting upright.

She nodded, lifting an arm draped with the outer garment. "It was getting too hot for this," she said, hanging it on the chair back.

"So today it's the Cerulean?" He smiled, settling back into the chair. "A beautiful bird but its numbers are rapidly decreasing. In fact, I've not seen a Cerulean since coming here. Have you?"

"Once," she said. "Even before having this shirt."

Given she was predisposed to odd behaviors and remarks, he dismissed this one. "Well, once is plenty for a rare bird. I've been working years for just one glimpse of a very special bird."

"The Ivory-billed Woodpecker?"

His smile went from low beam to high. "You know about that? Then you probably know that Glenn and I just got back from Arkansas. We were searching for the woodpecker in the Cache River Wildlife Refuge, where it was rediscovered in 2004."

"You didn't find it, though, huh?"

His smile acquired an odd twist. "No sighting; that's correct. But I've lots of video hours to watch yet. That's what I was doing when you "broke in.""

Noise from the riding mower competed with the hush of falling water. Robert stood, waving to Billy to cut the engine. "Get some tea before you start," he called down to the boy dismounting from the high mower. Then turning to Claire, asked. "You do have sun block and a hat to block the sun, right?"

She nodded emphatically, though in fact had forgotten all about it. Glenn returned, pushing through the patio gate, as the song of a distant bird brushed the air. Robert and Claire bent their heads to it.

"That's not a Field Sparrow, is it?" Claire asked.

"Shhhh!" said Robert.

zhee-zhee-zhee-zizizizi zzzeeeet
zhee-zhee-zhee-zizizizi zzzeeeet

Likewise in a listening posture, Glenn was first to speak after the bird stopped singing. "No, Claire. That's a Cerulean Warbler."

13

Mars at Last

As Victor's mother searched the house for the apron to her waitress uniform, Billy placed his laptop beside Victor's on the round kitchen table. Given the importance of the Mars landing, Rose permitted Billy to spend the day, even though it went against house rules. The boys, however, would not talk openly until she left. Victor still knew nothing of Billy's landscaping job for Crawley or Claire's partnership in that venture. He knew only that Claire had confided to Billy their knowledge of his fugitive father's hideout, which was much more than he wanted to know.

The two boys stood staring silently at one another while Rose, clutching a black apron trimmed in white, grabbed her car keys from the Formica counter.

"Good luck, boys," she said, stopping at the screen door to take a shallow, harried breath. "Let me know when you land."

Alone, neither boy spoke, each awaiting the other. Victor turned toward the refrigerator and yanked it open, speaking with his head inside. "Claire told me you know that we know about your father." He pulled out two cans of ginger ale and tossed one to Billy. "Now what?"

Billy caught the can and tossed it in the air. "Thanks, man, for not squealing."

An expression of gratitude was the last thing Victor expected. He stood, back to the open refrigerator door. "Sure."

"I was scared for a bit," Billy brushed the hair from his glass eye. "But he's leaving, so everything's cool."

"Your father's leaving?" Victor's tone rose hopefully.

"Yeah. Didn't Belle tell you?" Billy pulled out a maple-stained chair and sank onto it.

At once, the oddity of Billy's behaviors and appearance hit Victor: clean hair swept from his glass eye, a show of gratitude, and now this casual, almost intimate, reference to Claire, and by her last name. Somehow it seemed more intimate than using her first name. Victor pulled out a chair opposite Billy, dropped into it, and said, "Well, fill me in."

"Geez, Arquetana!" Billy scooted his chair across the linoleum floor to stretch a long leg toward the refrigerator door. "Are you goofy today, or what?" He pushed it shut with his foot.

Victor was shocked to learn that Claire had ridden with Billy—on his quad—to the Crawley chateau. And that she had agreed to work with him to earn money for his father was nothing less than bizarre. How could the entire world turn upside down in two days? He listened in disbelief as Billy described their workday together, a narrative filled with references to Claire, or as Billy now called her, Belle.

Victor felt uncomfortable; he didn't want to hear any more. The seat beneath his bottom felt too hard. He shifted this way and that before jumping up. "I'm hungry," he said, cutting off Billy. "What about you?" He opened the refrigerator door and Billy flew into it.

"I'll eat anything."

After devouring leftover pizza and banana and peanut butter sandwiches, the two prepared for "Mission Mind" —a serious focus on the task at hand. In less than 30 minutes, online access to the video game *Flight Fever* would be released to thousands of players in the United States and Europe. Having devised a "patch" for a programming error, the corporation FF Inc., also provided a one-month window within which all prior players could download the patch. That time window was shutting fast, with only moments to go. At noon Eastern Daylight Standard Time, the game would commence exactly where it "ended," that end point decided by a panel of game developers and ethicists. The chosen point was thirty minutes prior to the first team's failed attempt. Only moments from atmospheric entry, Victor and Billy wiped peanut butter from their fingers and mouths, and carted their laptops into the living room.

Front window drapery closed, phones off, the boys sat on overstuffed pillows, backs propped against the living room couch, legs beneath a low-rise coffee table. Laptops open, browser windows adjacent, headsets on, they breathed deeply. From a control panel clock, they counted down the seconds: 10, 9, 8, 7, 6, 5, 4, 3, 2, 1: the game commenced—thirty minutes out from entry trajectory.

The boys could now view their animated selves, and four other game-generated avatars (all six comprising the crew) seated within the vertical ascent/descent vehicle. To get here, at the edge of a fiery plunge into the thin Martian atmosphere, Victor and Billy had traveled in a crew transport craft from the orbit of Earth to the orbit of Mars. Now, months absent from the game, they were about to try again. Entry path angle and velocity, newly calculated by system computers, pointed the nose of the vehicle. The engines fired. Victor and Billy shared a desperate, expectant look.

Late in the morning of the next day, Claire drifted with a warm breeze to the pond, a man-made crater of shimmering emerald water. Tall grasses rimmed the pond separating it from the cultivated lawn. Within its tangle grew pretty ox-eye daisies and fleabane, pale pink rays around a bright yellow disk.

Sitting on haunches within this private world, she inhaled the sweet scent of mint covering a high bank. Everywhere orange-brown salamanders hung with limp limbs in the warm shallow water. Lowering to her stomach, she peered down and under the bank. Behind a curtain of falling water, in an inlet the size of a shovel spade, sat a frog, green and glistening.

Head hanging upside down, ears funneling the sound of water, Claire didn't expect a visitor. When an especially stealthy one stood straddling her prone figure, she had no idea.

When said visitor bent forward, index fingers pointing to either side of her rib cage, she was carelessly dipping her own fingers into the pond.

Poking digits dug into her sides. She heaved upward like a fish thrown from the water. Up and over, she flung onto her back, catching his legs with her own as he toppled to the ground beside her. "Victor!" she gasped. "You jerk!"

"I couldn't help it," he said, rolling onto his side. A happy grin flowed over his face, flooding his eyes. He planted an elbow into the ground to support his head and Claire scooted toward him.

"You never called last night." She arranged herself into a cross-legged sitting position. "I waited and waited to hear about the landing." Victor squinted into her lovely face framed in a halo of white hair. Against it, the sun-bleached sky looked vibrantly blue.

He sat likewise, their knees squared and touching. "I wanted to tell you in person," he said, attempting a dour expression, the better to surprise her. But the truth, triumphant and loud, shouted from his eyes.

"You did it!" Across their laps, she groped to hug him.

"We did!" he cried, bracing gentle arms over her shoulders. "We landed on Mars!"

Suddenly shy, they broke apart to stand. A welcomed distraction drew their eyes and ears: hawking crows, at least a dozen, descended into the tall walnut tree some 100 feet behind them. From within their noisy ranks, one large crow flew down to the lawn and waddled toward them. Below his right shoulder was a white patch. "Colonel White Badge!" Claire cried.

Victor shook his head in amazement. "Yeah. I see." Both glanced to her tee shirt appliqué of a life-sized blue-black American Crow. "Hey!" he said, darting from their bed of crushed grasses. "Let's see if he follows." Together they headed from the pond toward the back of the house, with Colonel White Badge waddling after.

"He probably wants something to eat." She stopped to look at the crow. "I don't have muffins today, Colonel," she said, bending forward, hands on knees.

"You gotta' be kidding," Victor said, his voice suddenly flat.

"What?" Claire turned to the sound of knuckles knocking against glass. Through the wall of windows in the summer kitchen, Louise excitedly waved to them. Beside her stood Robert Crawley.

"What does he want?" complained Victor as Louise escorted her guest down the length of the long room toward the back side door. Claire ignored him, too shocked to respond. She shuffled thoughtlessly toward the door. Colonel White Badge followed.

The colonel's troop took huge exception to this folly. They called out in alarm with shrill notes and rattles, some flapping to the ground. But the colonel took no heed, standing beside

Claire and watching, as she did, the back door. When suddenly it opened, the Colonel tripped into the air on crooked wings, pumping for lift. The tip of his wing brushed her forehead as he banked, flying toward the walnut tree.

Startled by the updraft of black wings, Louise pushed through the screen door. "What was that?"

Behind her, Robert squeezed out. Standing beside Louise, he looked short. "Just some crows," he answered, smiling at Claire. Robert wore a short-sleeved sapphire blue shirt, open collar, and white shorts. "But why they should crowd the back door . . . " he paused to scrutinize the poster-sized image of a crow stamped on her shirt. A sudden thought woke his slumbering brows that leap into his forehead.

Claire could not focus on her mother's words of introduction. She did not notice Victor, standing closely alongside her. All she could see was the astonishment in Robert's blazing blue eyes. She could see at once that he knew her secret. A kind of telepathy exchanged between them. His eyes interrogated her. They asked, "Is it true? Do you summon these birds somehow?" And with her eyes alone she answered, "Yes."

Within a sudden silence, Claire and Robert looked to Louise who stood waiting for some response but neither knew what she had said. Even Victor wasn't quite sure, distracted as he was by Mrs. Belle's odd demeanor. She appeared flustered, her face flushing rose, as she repeatedly sifted fingers through her chin-length sandy blond hair. Luckily, the impasse was broken by the wrecking crew of one English sheepdog and one aging but agile beagle.

First to slip through the screen door, that never properly closed, was Moon Doggy. He cut a path between Louise and Robert, causing the man to stumble. Bolting into his wake was Sammy. The sheepdog's swagger knocked Robert off his feet and onto the ground, hard. Mother and daughter shrieked with concern, falling to his assistance. Victor merely smirked, rubbing the knot of twisting dogs around his legs.

Robert landed on his right hip. Except for the grass stain on his white shorts and the purple bruise forming beneath, he was okay. Banishing the troublesome dogs to the backyard, Louise urged everyone into the storeroom. Claire drew back to let the others enter, straining to pick out Colonel White Badge from his regiment arranged as a wave of blue-black luster through the tree. A single crow, the colonel, dove from a high perch to land several feet from her. He waddled toward her so insistently that she stepped back. Raising his bill to the air, he scolded her in a rapid series of hoarse caws. Then flapping his glossy wings indignantly, he squawked, *Hurry!*

14

Time to Fly

The next day, and every day thereafter for over a week, Robert Crawley arrived at the store, always after Jerry's departure to visit Ben in the hospital. His announced reason was for the pie and coffee special. Louise, though, couldn't help suspect he came to visit her, an exciting prospect. Since her husband's death, she had dated only once, a couple years earlier. But the man had not interested her. No one had interested Louise but her daughter. Yet at 31, she was still a young, attractive woman.

Claire felt jealous of her mother because Robert directed his attention mostly to Louise. Even so, with each visit he reserved one covert glance for her alone that spoke of their common, unspoken knowledge.

As word spread of the billionaire's morning routine, more locals began to arrive for the special. While Louise and Claire kept busy attending to their orders, Robert Crawley, world famous ornithologist, kept busy entertaining. It began with the skinny teen who entered the store on Robert's first morning visit. Chewing gum loudly, she had asked, "Who owns that freaky car?" Thereafter, Robert's SUV stood in the lot as a sign for all to read: "The ornithologist is in." And in they came. To accommodate their numbers, Louise stuffed the crowded floor with additional foldout tables and chairs. Of course, each evening, Jerry had to bake more pies, something he enjoyed grumbling about.

The first curious few to stop by Robert's table asked about his outlandish car. These exchanges sometimes led to conversations, which each time the ornithologist steered to one destination: his search for the Ivory-billed Woodpecker. Most people, having never heard of the exotic bird, wanted to hear more. Grabbing the closest chair, they'd order the special, urging Crawley to tell his story.

He told of a black-and-white woodpecker, 20 inches in length with a flaming-red crest and long ivory-colored bill. A bird of the southeast and Cuba, this woodpecker—largest in the United States—once lived in the bottomland hardwood forests. There it fed on insects and beetle larvae from dead and dying trees. He described the bird's call and its unique "double-knock" drumming sound.

"But after the Civil War, to clear land, the South logged its hardwood forests," Robert would say, repeating the same words each day as if from a script. "And to escape the destruction, the Ivory-bill had to retreat." Here he would pause, waiting for the inevitable question.

"To where?" someone always asked.

Turning to the questioner slowly, he'd tilt his head and lift one brow: "To its last haven and hope—the swamplands."

So intriguing was Robert's opening "hook" that Charles B. Must, local paper reporter, asked to use it. Two days later, *The*

Chapter 14

Tipple Daily News printed a front-page story. In the article, Must explained the continual decline of the woodpecker's habitat. How in the late 1930's, the last remaining Ivory-bills (maybe two dozen) were believed to inhabit a large tract of primeval forest in Louisiana. Valiant efforts by the National Audubon Society to preserve the forest failed. And in the aftermath of the destruction, an envoy found a single woodpecker in a small, insolated stand of remaining trees.

Like everyone else in the community, Claire hungrily read the article, hoping to learn some stray details of Robert Crawley. Taking the paper to read in her bedroom, she wasn't prepared for its tragic details of extermination, particularly not the shooting of a pair of Ivory-bills in Florida (1924) by two local taxidermists. The fact stung her eyes. They burned and began bleeding tears. With the sound of newspaper crunching under chest, she slid off her bed into a crumpled heap on the floor and cried.

She cried for Mr. Buteo, the Red-tailed Hawk shot by Clyde Hollow and then stuffed by some local taxidermist. The proud male hawk had been Ku-Khain's mate, though at that time Claire knew the female as Big Red. She vividly remembered how Billy reveled in her horror to see the magnificent male raptor frozen in death. Mounted upon a stand, posed with wings unfolding, he was set at the edge of a stainless steal table in a metal shed. She shuddered to think of it. Yet here she was, helping Billy to help his father to escape the law. How could she have forgotten poor Mr. Buteo?

Claire didn't finish the article but jumped up, resolved that minute to visit Ku-Khain. Sammy, lying forgotten in the summer kitchen, heard her pounding footsteps through the walls and ceiling of the house. She was heading out—and so then was he! The sheepdog met her at the front door, tail pumping at full power, ready to charge the world. Claire paused, hand on knob: "Should we get Moon Doggy?"

Cocking his head as dogs do, the sheepdog looked into her face. His large black nose quivering, his eyes straining for a gesture or sound that meant—"Let's go!"

"Okay, Sammy—just you and me!" She yanked open the door, happy for an outing like old times. On the store side of the divided porch stood Mrs. Miller, a short, stout woman with hair like a skullcap, about to enter the store.

"Did I miss Mr. Crawley, then?" she asked in a voice as blunt as her face.

"Left hours ago," Claire called, hurrying to outrun the woman's next question. A hearty breeze chased girl and dog across the road and through the meadow to a tall stand of poplars shimmying in the wind. Claire entered the woodland, trying to dislodge Mr. Buteo from a perch in her mind. But he clung to it with the tenacity of death. As a distraction, she called to Sammy, below at the creek. "Wait for me, boy!"

Before wading into his favorite pool, the sheepdog looked back. The swivel of his head and the swagger of his hind end both said, "I don't think so." He plunged into the cold water, lapping it with gusto.

Claire hurried down the incline, mindful of every stumbling point—the exposed rocks, foot-sized holes, and fallen limbs of trees. All circumvented. She arrived at the water hole as Sammy emerged on its other side, his glorious full-plumed tail now a boney strip strung with wet, sagging fur. A quick shake and he bounded up the hill through a noble stand of mature hemlock.

She sighed, smiling. Sammy's utter joy always made her feel better. She stepped across the creek on half-submerged rocks, slipping off one. She headed up the hill with one soggy shoe, inhaling the humid, sweet smell of the woodland.

Her mind drifted to Ku-Khain and the night she saved the hawk from a snare set by Clyde Hollow. To lift the raptor free from the trap, she had offered her forearm wrapped in a sweatshirt. The large, yet incredibly light bird, pierced the fabric with the talons of one claw, the other hanging limp behind, strangled in monofilament line. While Claire unwound the line, the hawk patiently waited. When done, she thrust out her arm and Ku-Khain heaved upward, as a diver springing off a board. Into the night her wings unfolded, grappling for lift, and then she was gone.

Everyone Claire told of that night found it incredible that a hawk, even one in distress, could be so docile on her arm. She, however, understood it to be a consequence of their spiritual bond and still did. Yet now a practical explanation also existed: Ku-Khain *knew* the perch of a human arm. She learned it at an early age, when the arm extended belonged to Robert Crawley, when her name, given by him, was Alexandra.

Claire walked a corridor of thoughts, heedless of the hiding sun or the playing wind, enticing the trees to motion. She raised a forearm to imagine her beloved hawk perched upon it. Ku-Khain would never more be hers alone. Robert Crawley had his own claim. The idea made her feel possessive; she didn't want to share Ku-Khain with Robert. That she shared the hawk with Victor was different. On their visits to the nest, Victor came as a guest, knowing full well that Ku-Khain was *her* family, not his. Lowering her arm, she continued through a grove of mature hemlock.

She had told Robert the story of how Ku-Khain found her, as a toddler lost in the woods, to impress him. And she would have told him more—everything—if not for Victor, who insisted they keep the female Red-tail a secret from the billionaire. And now she was glad of it.

The gusting wind felt wonderful against her skin. In a clearing she stood with arms outstretched and face lifted skyward. Continents of gray rain clouds had formed during her walk through the woodland. The rain was imminent; she'd have to hurry. Through the mountain laurel, whose pedals littered the ground like summer snow, she strode toward a line of white pine trees. Behind these trees, the earth's soft, scented flesh yielded to its bone—rocky appendages reaching above a narrow valley. Before heading on, she scanned for Sammy, who was nowhere about. She passed through the white pine and climbed atop the Fist.

The wind began to subside as Claire took position, squatting on the north edge of the rock table. Facing north provided a straight-line view to the hawk's nest, set in an alcove on the rock face of the Finger. Across the breach of open space she could plainly see the nest, which looked empty. Alarmed she focused her binoculars. It was empty but for one fledgling, lying low in the nest with his head propped atop the nest edge. The wind whipped the down of his head. She stood upright. Where were the others? She strode to the eastern edge of the rock table, scanning the sky over the valley. A gray expanse of low, fast moving clouds seemed to sweep her up, as in a swift moving sea. The sensation disoriented her. Away from the edge, she stumbled backward.

From the south, Ku-Khain flew suddenly by the Fist, a lifeless young rabbit in her grip. She dove toward the Finger and the nest but did not land. With mighty beating wings, she tread the air, dangling the meal before her offspring. He lurched upward, flapping his wings for lift, almost falling over the edge.

Claire gasped.

Ku-Khain flew off to circle back, riding an updraft past the nest. Again, the fledgling lurched, furiously flapping toward the dangling bait, just as an updraft lifted him. Buoyed by the wind, wings outstretched, the hawk took his first soaring flight—directly to the ground below. He landed at the base of the Fist, against the broken shale and scrub vegetation. Claire fell to her knees, crawling to look over the edge. She watched as Ku-Khain swooped down, dropping the rabbit to him.

Immediately the hungry bird pounced upon his dearly earned food. Hunching over his meal, spreading his wings like a shield to hide it from view, the hawk began to feed. Claire then understood: she was witness to the last of Ku-Khain's brood to fledge.

Claire made it home before the rain and headed to her bedroom with Sammy. Moon Doggy found them en route through the living room, eager to smell on the sheepdog's fur everything he had missed. He crowded them on the winding steps, indignant at having been left behind. Through the open windows of her bedroom came the sound of pounding rain against the tin roof. She plopped back on the bed, inhaling its sweet scent. Moon Doggy jumped up with her and Sammy slumped to the rug, exhausted and ready for a much-needed rest. Staring up at the ceiling, Claire let her mind drift.

On the trip back from the outcrop, she had heard the drumming of a woodpecker and suspected the Red-bellied because its image beckoned from her shirtfront. When the woodpecker called its rolling *Kwirr,* she knew: Red-bellied. She no longer pondered the mystery of her ability to draw in birds; she simply did. Of late, a different enigma absorbed

133

Chapter 14

her—the word *Hurry!* Why did she imagine birds to be calling it to her? It had been easy to forget this word shouted within a dream. And flight of fancy might account for her translation of the towhee's alarm call. But how could she explain the most recent envoy's squawked imperative? Colonel White Badge's message to her was clear—*Hurry!* Not clear, however, was to where or about what she should hurry.

The newspaper read and discarded earlier that day still lay on the bed, crunching beneath her back. She sat up to finish the article, which told of the sightings in 2004 and 2005 of the Ivory-billed Woodpecker, long believed to be extinct. She read of the expeditions, coalitions of conservation and birding groups to find the woodpecker, and finally of Robert Crawley's most recent failed attempt. Her hands dropped and the newspaper sagged. Claire bounced from the bed so urgently that Moon Doggy dove with her, directly onto Sammy who, awoken suddenly, clumsily heaved upward.

"Of course!" she shouted to the dogs, watching her eagerly for their instructions. "The Ivory-bill will come to me!" She wrestled the top drawer of her desk for some paper and a pen and sat at the desk to write.

"I'll tell him with a note," she told the dogs, who now understood they were going nowhere. Moon Doggy jumped back up to the bed and Sammy slumped down to the rug. "I'll explain everything. Then maybe he'll take me to Arkansas to find the woodpecker."

15

The Note

Claire didn't think about what to say in her note; the pen
simply raced across the paper:

Dear Robert,
I think I can help you find the Ivory-
billed Woodpecker. Jerry says I keep birds in
my heart and that makes them come to me.
And it's true. I love birds and whenever I
want to see or hear one in particular, I
wear a t-shirt with that bird's image. Today
I'm wearing a Red-bellied Woodpecker and
I heard one in the woods, which made me
think about the Ivory-bill—I could draw
that woodpecker to me, too!
Please don't tell my mother I wrote this
note, but I want to help you. Besides, I want
to be an ornithologist like you one day.

Your Friend,
Claire

On Saturday, Claire served Robert his morning special with her note pressed against the plate bottom, jutting past the edge. Robert plucked the folded paper free from her fingers, looking up. "Is this yours?" he said, meaning to give it back.

Claire shook her head 'no,' glancing back to locate her mother, who stood retrieving another pie from the glass display. "It's a message for you," she whispered, looking only to the table where she set his pie and coffee. She did not look for his reaction but scurried away.

Sunday morning was spent with Jerry in the vegetable garden combating common chickweed. Even Becky played a part, scratching at the roots of the sprawling plant. Meanwhile, Patty perched within the grove of cherry trees, enjoying the company of her wild brethren. In good spirits since his friend's unexpected recovery, Jerry whistled while pulling weeds. His razor-sharp notes sliced Claire's eardrums until she could stand it no longer. "Could you stop whistling, please," she said belligerently. "I can't hear the birds."

"Not sure I want to stop whistling, Miss Sour Puss." He stood from a bent position to stretch, grunting loudly.

"You're doing that to aggravate me," she said, yanking a fistful of chickweed from the ground. When he chuckled, she glowered at him from her position stooped among mounds of cucumbers.

"Since you're in such a bad mood, I'm doing myself a favor." He brushed his hands of dirt, stepping out from among the crowded tomato plants. "You finish weeding. I'm going to sit by the pond and read the Sunday paper."

Claire sprang up. "I can't do all this myself!"

"Come on, Becky," he called to his hen, ignoring her protest. "Let's find a more pleasant atmosphere."

"Jerry!" she bellowed to his retreating form.

"Fine." He threw a hand into the air. "Do what you can now and finish tomorrow morning. Since school's out, you got nothing but time."

Claire stomped angrily through the mounded cucumbers, cutting across the garden toward the hillside. Patty flushed from the trees to avoid the storm plodding beneath and flew to the haven of Jerry's shoulder. Claire was in a foul mood. How could she help but be? She had confided her secret—not just any secret but the most important truth about herself—to Robert Crawley. Whatever made her do such a stupid thing? She grabbed a low brittle branch from the nearest tree bending it back until it snapped. A female Common Yellowthroat chipped in alarm before flying out and away. Claire turned to drop onto her bottom and fall back against the wet, morning ground. The green leaves above shimmered with sunlight. Three people now knew her secret—Jerry, Victor, and Robert. "Ooooohhhhh!" she wailed aloud, paddling her feet against the ground.

Jerry had been the first to find out, early in the spring, when she let the information slip out, quite accidentally. Until

137

Chapter 15

that moment, she had told no one, not even her mother, not ever her grandmother, or Mamo. She feared doing so, thinking her strange ability was an enchantment or spell of some kind that if spoken of would disappear. But Jerry had suggested a different explanation entirely, one that couldn't be "broken" so long as she loved birds. He said that she kept birds in her heart and that they were drawn to her because of it. And it made sense, especially since what she feared most—losing her ability—never happened.

Thereafter, she felt compelled to share with her best friend this wondrous truth: *anyone* could keep birds in his or her heart! The idea fascinated Victor and he became more interested in birds. Everything had been perfect—until now. Now that Robert knew, something felt terribly wrong.

The following gray morning, Robert did not come for the morning special, scrumptiously scenting the air with cinnamon, nutmeg, and baked apple. Each time the door swung open, Claire cringed, too embarrassed to look. The locals, however, did look and so expectantly that all conversation stopped until the newcomer, once noted, was collectively dismissed. Among those let down was Louise. With every opening of the door, her face rose hopefully only to quickly deflate, again and again.

With the last of the morning customers gone, Louise stood at the register organizing the money drawer. The day outside the large pane window looked like a dingy gray sheet. Claire and Jerry worked in the summer kitchen washing dishes and so didn't hear another customer pull into the empty lot. Louise heard the crunching gravel under rolling tires but couldn't be bothered to glance out the window. She was feeling foolish for her schoolgirl fascination with Robert Crawley. That morning, she had worn eye makeup, applied so lightly as not to be noticeable—or so she hoped. Maybe everyone noticed. With a hard shove, she shut the cash drawer, shaking her head.

Outside, a parrot-painted SUV shouted its colors so loudly that Louise finally looked. As Robert pushed through the entrance door, she had just enough time to smooth her hair.

Fifteen minutes later Jerry and Claire strolled from the summer kitchen into the store unaware of the billionaire's brief visit. Louise stood from her seat at the break table, brushing the front of her sunny yellow bib apron. She glanced at the floor, clamping her lips to suppress the smile dimpling her cheeks.

"What happened?" Jerry asked, smiling. Seeing her pleasure he anticipated good news.

"Don't cut into a new one, Claire," Louise called to her daughter, retrieving a pie from the mahogany case. Louise stepped past Jerry to open the door of the summer kitchen closed on the dogs. They flooded through the threshold like a spigot on high. Jerry knew something was up since Louise didn't like dogs in the storeroom. She seemed to be stalling. It occurred to him then that Crawley might be involved.

"Claire, bring me a piece, too," he said, deciding to take a disinterested approach. He sat down at the break table where both dogs swarmed his legs. "Need coffee," he muttered, heaving up to lead the dogs to and through the swinging door into the living room. Louise grabbed a fresh pot and met Jerry with it and a mug back at the break table.

Claire hastily dropped two plates of pie onto the table. "Let's eat fast before we get another customer," she said, sitting and stoking her mouth with the first fork load.

"Well, you won't believe it," Louise said, standing over them, coffee pot clutched in hand.

"I'll believe it, just tell us already," Jerry said, in a teasing, good-natured sort of way. His true attitude was much more critical.

"Robert Crawley just left—"

"Robert was here!" Claire blurted, pounding a fist on the table. "Why didn't you get us?"

Jerry pulled out a chair. "Put down that pot, Louise, and sit down. You're making me nervous."

Louise sat down, tucking sandy blond hair behind one ear. "Before you get too excited," she looked directly into Claire's insistent, blazing eyes. "I said, 'no.'" Then she glanced toward Jerry but did not meet his critical gaze. "Robert invited us all—you included, Jerry—for a weekend outing to the White River National Wildlife Refuge."

"What?" Claire shot upward, knocking the table and spilling Jerry's coffee. "You can't say 'no'! It's to find the Ivory-billed Woodpecker!"

On the other side of the swinging door, Sammy and Moon Doggy began wailing in response to Claire's shrill outburst. Wiping the spill with napkins, Jerry muttered loudly to be heard above the noise. "The nerve of that guy. First Ben and now this." He shook his wooly head in dismay.

"Stop it!" Louise shouted, pushing up and away from the table. She hollered toward the living room. "All of you!" and the dogs went quiet as did her two critics. "I told you both, I said 'no,' so forget it." She marched toward the swinging door, pushing through with a force equal to her explosive mood. Claire and Jerry looked to one another sheepishly.

While Louise hid in her bedroom, Jerry and Claire skulked in the storeroom like scolded pups. Both felt guilty but neither could reject their own churning emotions. Jerry was infuriated that Robert Crawley could so quickly insinuate himself into their lives. Who was he anyway? Just a self-important, privileged boy who thought the world owed him everything. That Louise, ordinarily a sensible woman, should fall for this man's empty "charms" galled Jerry like a boil on the butt.

Claire couldn't long contain her agitation. She vented her protests to Jerry, a totally unsympathetic ear since he thought a weekend trip to Arkansas a preposterous idea. "But it's to find the Ivory-billed Woodpecker," she whined, doggedly tracking him from the storeroom into the summer kitchen. He clattered the tins on a shelf above the iron woodstove, searching for his favorite pie pan.

Chapter 15

"If that dang fool wanted to ask her out, then why not simply take her to dinner?" he said, ignoring Claire's concerns. "No, he concocts some bigger than life adventure," he swept the air with the selected tin, "—just to impress her."

"Would you listen to me!" Claire nearly screamed. Though Jerry looked directly at her, she could see a mental screen tightly shut behind his hazel eyes. If only she could tell him the real reason for their invitation. Robert needed *her*—not her mother and not him—to go to the White River. The Ivory-billed Woodpecker would come out of hiding for her alone, no one else. "You don't have to go if you don't want," she said, pleading. "But why can't I go?"

At the other end of the room, stepping down into the summer kitchen, Louise startled them. "Because a little girl cannot travel alone with a grown man. End of story."

"But you can go, too!" Toward her mother Claire flew, a bottle-nosed fly prepared to zoom her target relentlessly.

"I can't go and I don't want to. And if we go anywhere this year, it'll be to Ireland to see your Mamo. So drop it right now." A more deliberate pronouncement could not have been made.

Claire knew enough to drop the subject, at least for the moment. Over the next couple days, she studiously argued an alternative—one hatched while complaining to Victor on the phone. Though no fan of Crawley's, Victor was gripped by the idea of searching for a rare bird in the bayous of the "Big Woods" of Arkansas. Equally fascinating was the probable mode of transportation. "I bet he has a private jet," Victor had said. "Wouldn't that be too cool to fly down on his jet?"

Claire hadn't even thought about the trip down. Her imagination painted only one picture: an Ivory-billed Woodpecker sweeping down toward her from some high branch in an ancient baldcypress tree. "Yeah, that would be cool," she said, unconvincingly. Then, quite unexpectedly, a solution struck.

"Victor!" she had shouted so loudly into the phone that he pulled it from his ear. "What if you were to come—and your dad? Then I wouldn't be traveling alone with a grown man. I'd be traveling with you and a parent!" Victor didn't have to be convinced. He readily agreed to pitch the idea to his father.

To Claire's amazement, her mother did not immediately shut down the idea of a trip to Arkansas with Victor and George Arquetana. Everyone in Tipple knew and respected George, as did Louise. She had no qualms about assuring her daughter's safety to him. (After all, he was the man who found Claire when lost in the woods.) And doubting that George could—or would—go, Louise agreed to the idea in theory. At least then Claire would stop pestering her.

But Louise lost the gamble. Only hours after giving her conditional consent, she received a phone call from Victor's father. He thanked her for the opportunity and her trust in him to safeguard Claire. "Of course, we'll never see the Ivory-bill, but it will be great fun to try," he said with exuberance.

Louise cleared her throat. "I'm sure it will be, but—" She stalled, not quite sure how to explain. "I don't know that there still is a trip. Mr. Crawley originally invited Claire, Jerry, and me, but I declined. Otherwise, Claire has masterminded this new outing with Victor and you. I don't think Mr. Crawley even knows about it."

Mr. Arquetana accepted this news with good humor. "That's kids for you." And Louise could imagine the wide smile born of his quiet chuckle. "They see only the possibilities in life. But so long as there is one, Victor and I are definitely interested. Just let us know," he said.

Clearing this misunderstanding with George was a relief for Louise. Like Jerry, she believed that Robert's offer, though extended to her family, was intended for her alone. So almost certainly there'd be no trip to Arkansas, and she felt badly for her daughter's upcoming disappointment.

But two days later, Louise stood at the store entrance, waving goodbye to Clare, Victor, and George climbing into Robert's Crawley's SUV. Robert sat in the driver's seat, smiling and waving back. They were en route to the University Park Airport, in State College, Pennsylvania, where a private jet and two pilots waited to fly the foursome to Stuttgart, Arkansas. Louise waved, smiling, still shaking her head in disbelief and no little trepidation.

16

To the Grand Prairie

Claire and Victor darted ahead of the men walking briskly across the tarmac toward the waiting aircraft. Several hundred feet beyond sat a pearl white private jet glistening in the sun. Seven cabin windows lined the fuselage tracking three ruby red stripes. All stopped to survey this marvel of engineering soon to transport them high above the world. Toward the open hatch the young pair sprinted.

The jet taxied to the runway where it began to accelerate, tarmac rolling into a blur. Engines whirred to a screaming pitch and the ground fell away. Aloft, the jet quickly gained altitude. Woodlands appeared as manicured shrubs within a landscape of cornrows and lanky, flowing wheat. Still higher and the earth became a vast swath of beige, brown, and green patches. Then they were gazing down at a layer of pearly clouds stretching to the horizon and hiding the world below. Above a vaporous expanse of soft, curling swells they glided, citizens of some celestial realm. Within a blue, featureless atmosphere, a single star blazed supreme. Claire stared out the window, inhaling the scene into her soul.

From the deep comfort of his over-stuffed leather chair, Robert stood to announce a surprise for his guest (similarly seated about a circular coffee table): tee shirts with a silkscreen image of the striking Ivory-billed Woodpecker.

Claire clutched the shirt extended her, beaming at the ornithologist. Though all received a shirt, hers was the one that mattered for hers alone was the task to draw in the woodpecker.

"The secret to identifying the Ivory-bill," said Robert, looking to Claire, "is not to confuse it with the Pileated." He pulled from a leather satchel colored posters with which to illustrate the physical differences between the common Pileated and the rare, elusive Ivory-bill—both large, black and white birds with flaming red crests.

Sitting on the edge of his seat, Robert reviewed their differences. "For instance, the male's red crest is pointed, not bushy like the Pileated's, and starts farther back on the forehead. Its bill is ivory, not dark. But most importantly the trailing edge of the Ivory-bill's wing is white, not black." Elaborating on several distinguishing details, he dismissed them just as quickly. "The ONLY thing I want you to focus on is the amount and distribution of white plumage." He stared directly at Claire. "And why?"

Startled, straining to think beyond the image of his loose curls and brilliant blue eyes, she said, "Because the other details are too small to see when the bird is in flight?"

Exhaling a long satisfied breath, Robert leaned back into his chair. "Exactly!"

They landed at the Stuttgart Airport, descending from the air-conditioned jet into heavy, hot air. The noon sun licked

Claire's pale skin like a sticky tongue. Squinting from the
metallic blaze of planes and vehicles, the group hurried into an
awaiting SUV. George took the driver's seat and everyone
plunged into the cool, shaded interior. Before hitting the open
road, they stopped at a diner, its plate glass windows shaded
by bamboo screens. Down a long lunch counter, diners
swiveled on their seats to inspect the new arrivals.

"Back again, Crawley?" said a ruddy-faced senior,
chortling. His neighbor, a withered man, hair plastered to an
age-spotted skull, chimed in. "That woodpecker gotcha on a
short leash?" Others chuckled at the ribbing given their "pet"
billionaire, visiting with his latest entourage. Robert accepted
their comments good-naturedly while leading his group to an
overlarge booth, across from the kitchen pick-up window.
Victor slid into a high-backed vinyl seat beside Claire.

A young woman with mousy hair and large hazel eyes
hurriedly approached, carrying smells of searing beef. She
spoke to Robert with the embarrassed merriment of someone
harboring a deep crush. All but he keenly listened to her self-
conscious ramblings, ranging in every note of the octave.
Stopping suddenly, she tucked hair strands behind a blushing
ear. "I'm right addled today for some reason," she said but
quickly composed herself to offer the day's "plate" special.

Claire alone did not order the plate special: chicken-fried
steak, mashed potatoes, and collard greens. Mostly vegetarian,
she opted for stewed tomatoes, baked macaroni and cheese,

with a side of Coleslaw. When all were finished eating, Robert pushed aside the plates and pulled a folded brochure from his back pocket, slapping it onto the table. "Inside there's a map of the refuge. Go ahead, open it."

Dutifully Claire grabbed and opened the brochure into a large rectangular map of the long, narrow refuge divided into north and south units. All that remained of a once vast forest of bottomland hardwoods was a wooded corridor hugging either side of the White River.

"Look closely," Robert urged, as Victor slid beside Claire to scan the map. "The refuge is 90 miles long and varies in width from three to ten miles. I've been on nearly every lake, bay, and bayou." He leaned forward. "So I was thinking," he looked from Claire to Victor. "Why not let you two decide?"

Claire gagged on the last slurp of sweet tea in her straw. She coughed to clear air from her esophagus while Victor slapped her back. Tears welling, she squeaked, "You want *us* to decide?"

Robert nodded, connecting his startling blue eyes with hers, sending the unspoken message (*I want YOU to decide*). She grabbed the map and slid out of the booth with Victor right behind. "We'll wait in the car," she called, knowing that Robert wanted *her* to decide because she alone could summon the secretive Ivory-bill.

Claire and Victor sat as sentinels at their backseat windows. Beyond the town limits, they drove south over roads straight as runway strips through deep alternating fields of rice, soybean, or cotton, not a farmhouse or barn in sight. The vast, flat landscape, known historically as the Grand Prairie, flowed free of territorial claim except for industrial silos, grouped into large complexes, most for storing and drying rice.

The two-lane highway to Crockett's Bluff, a small community perched above the White River, ran as straight as any ruler. In the distance, a hot road "mirage" melted asphalt into the horizon. And everywhere the tumbling blue sky fell to deep fields of vibrant green rice, like knee-high grass. Where the highway began to wind and fields gave way to wooded lots, they pulled off the road onto a dirt lane and over a rickety wooden bridge to access an overlook of the wide caramel-colored river. After a brief study, including rock-dropping measures of its distance below (maybe forty feet) and estimates of its width (some four hundred) they piled back into the car.

"Now," said Robert, taking his turn at the driver's seat, "Who wants to see some Snowy Egrets?" Starting the ignition, he twisted back to Claire, nodding with a glance to the plumed egret, a blaze of white against her navy tee shirt (a present from her Mamo in Ireland). "I suspect there's at least one in our number who'd be interested."

Victor dove toward Claire's ear to implant there an accusation. "You told him our secret!"

Annoyed at his presumption—after all it was *her* secret to share, not his—Claire resisted the truth. "Think what you want," she said, shoving him away.

They drove less than a mile to where the narrow road crossed a marshy inlet. Even from their window seats, on the road above the marsh, they could see a small array of egrets, Great and Snowy. The bright white birds, elegant and dreamlike in the hazy air, stood poised in shallow water. Possessing slender, long necks and stick-like legs, the Great Egrets were the taller, standing as high as a yardstick, their bills sturdy and yellow. Yet by comparison the Snowy Egrets did not disappoint. A foot shorter, they too boasted graceful swan-like necks but with slender black bills and a spray of curving plumes over their lower back and neck.

Robert parked up the road so as not to disturb the perfect tableau of avian angels. For that is how they appeared to Claire, too pure, too delicate to be earthly. But these white herons were in fact merciless hunters, patient and lethal.

Claire hurried to Robert's side as the group walked the quiet road toward the inlet. Behind them, Victor strained to hear their conversation while maintaining one with his father. Nearing the small asphalt bridge, they stepped gently to watch from a low concrete wall. The four Snowy and three Great Egrets did not acknowledge their assembling audience. Each stood absorbed in the hunt for crawfish, salamander, frog, or other unlucky water critter. Neck extended over the water, yellow bill poised, a Great Egret jabbed the gray-green surface and retrieved a small, struggling snake. Head trumpeting skyward, he opened a gaping beak and the reptile disappeared.

Claire smacked her bare arm. "Ouch! Something just stung me!" She cried too loudly, for the egrets, now aroused, extended their alabaster wings and ascended into the sky, levitated by heaven itself. Claire screeched, stumbling back and swapping the air. "Mosquitoes!" She jogged toward the car to outrun her pursuers. Victor found this amusing and chased after.

"Great!" he called after her. "Maybe you've got a new power—to attract bugs!" But she ignored his spiteful laughter, grabbing the car door handle.

From Highway 153, they drove east on Highway 1, heading toward the wildlife refuge office and visitor center. Once there, Claire and Victor dove from the air-conditioned car into the broiling afternoon. Across the nearly empty parking lot, rippling with heat, they raced toward the glass doors of the center, a charring sun chasing after. Escaping its glare, they pushed into the cool lobby, sighing aloud.

The central floor held a huge exhibit of a baldcypress tree onto which a black bear family climbed. Though the tree was synthetic the bears were real—a mother and her cubs—long dead and stuffed. An image of Mr. Buteo filling her mind, Claire pouted. "I hate that they stuff real animals for these displays."

"Never use that word, Claire," Victor said emphatically.

"What word?"

A woman's voice intruded. "I bet I know what word."

Both turned to see a slender, young black woman, wearing khaki shirt and pants, standing alongside them. Neither could think to respond, still absorbing her presence. She stood a few inches taller than Claire. A halo of tiny, glistening curls rose from a rhinestone-studded hair comb beyond the hairline of a high forehead. Finely etched brows followed the upward slant of large, dark eyes. The woman raised these brows in expectation.

"You do?" asked Victor, absorbed by the tiny diamond studding her nose. Claire stared unabashedly at the woman, fascinated. Everything about her visage glistened or glittered, from the hair comb and diamond stud to the polished lips and bronze complexion.

"Sure I do. As a child, my daddy always told me never to use the word 'hate.'"

"But why?" asked Claire. "It's just a word."

The ranger looked to Victor to complete what he had begun. "Because words have power and 'hate' is particularly powerful."

Intrigued by the idea, Claire wasn't ready to concede. "But not if you use it innocently, to say something like, 'I hate broccoli.'"

Victor's response was agitated. "But you don't really *hate* broccoli, only dislike it. There's no uglier word than *hate,* but people—" he paused to indict her personally, "use it thoughtlessly all the time."

Claire felt somewhat put upon, eager now to defend herself. But before she could, Robert called out from the lobby entrance. "Zondra! I see you've met my young friends."

Introductions ensued after which Robert excluded these same 'young friends,' claiming the ranger's attention entirely for himself. Even Victor's father stood relegated to observer as the pair animatedly chatted. Given this, George directed his son into the bookstore while Claire drifted to the other side of the exhibit, her hands 'walking' its rail. She pretended to investigate the underwater diorama of fish and turtles, at the base of the tree, while tuning her ears to their conversation.

"I'm letting the kids choose where we search tomorrow," he said, in a self-congratulatory boast. "It's a big thrill for them."

Claire felt her face burn.

"Robert, those children need help to decide." Zondra spoke in a patronizing way, like mother to child. "Since you're here, why not suggest Moon Lake and Indian Bayou?"

Instantly Robert called for everyone's attention, drawing Victor and his father from a rolling display of postcards. Claire approached cautiously, eyes already wide with anticipation of what he would say and a complaint already formed to contest it. "But it was supposed to be our decision!" she cried, before Robert had finished parroting Zondra's suggestion. She turned anxiously to Victor, expecting his vocal support, but preferring to pay her back for the earlier slight, he simply shrugged. "Moon Lake sounds pretty cool to me."

17

Moon Lake

Moments later found them back on the highway traveling southwest to their night's accommodation, a one-room schoolhouse converted to a duck lodge. Roadside ditches, brimming with the water of a wet spring, glinted silver and yellow under the sun's glare.

Along Highway 276, within the community of Bayou Meto, they found the Schoolhouse Lodge: a rectangular white building with an orange roof embraced by more deep green fields of rice. Claire was first to pounce upon the wide, sun-baked deck running its length and wrapping about its back. Directly behind the lodge a large pond gleamed under the late afternoon sun. The air shimmered with birdsong. Red-winged Blackbirds called, sang, and whistled. *Conk-la-ree!*

"They're everywhere," gushed Claire, jogging toward the embankment with Victor right behind. Stopping to survey the expanse, they spotted and then sprinted to a finger of land poking into the pond. Four white Adirondack chairs arranged at its tip beckoned them. To lay first claim, they raced, laughing and jostling for position. Claire led the way, being first to plop into a chair. A rosy flush shone from her face, neck, and arms. Against damp temples clung a fringe of wavy white hair.

"So many redwings," said Victor, lifting heavy hair from the nape of his neck. "I'll tell you something you don't know."

"I bet I know more than you."

"This isn't about birds, Tahwach," he said, annoyed with her self-absorption. "It's about me. My Flight Fever avatar is RedWing." That she did not understand further exasperated him. "An *avatar* is the character that portrays you in a video game." He shook his head at her ignorance, drawing from his front pocket a band to pull back his hair. "In our Mars mission, my name is RedWing."

"What's Billy's avatar?" asked Claire.

Without comment, Victor sprang from his chair to head back to the lodge. "What?" she called after him, hoisting herself up. "What did I say?"

While the others showered, Robert busily worked preparing their evening meal with groceries purchased at a Piggly Wiggly® on the drive down. The smell of batter-fried fish was so enticing that even Claire, typically vegetarian, was eager to eat it. One by one Robert's guests emerged from their quaint rustic rooms with plank wood walls and colorful cotton quilts into the dining area, where a large American flag draped the back wall. On a dining table, the host had arranged their savory evening meal: lightly breaded filets of catfish, golden brown hush puppies, freshly steamed green beans, corn on the cob, and Coleslaw. All ate heartily and thereafter retired to the pond to watch an inflated red-orange sun sink below the horizon.

Later still while George and Robert watched part of a baseball game in the great room, Victor visited with Claire in her room. Sprawling on stomachs, each claimed one of the twin beds, situated in a diagonal on opposite walls. Oriented to the bottom of their beds, faces only feet apart, they spoke barely above a whisper. Claire rocked side to side on forearms to get comfortable. "Your father hardly ever talks. He's so quiet."

Victor's dark eyes filled with a strong, critical current. He pushed upward from his stomach to sit on his knees. "If your boyfriend would ever shut up maybe my father could talk."

Claire giggled because it was true. "He does like the sound of his voice," she agreed.

Pacified, Victor settled back down, prepared again to be confidants, yet not without complaint. "I still can't believe you told Crawley about your power with birds. Why would you do such a thing?" In her nervous blink, he obtained a confession. "I knew it," he fumed.

In no mood to defend herself, Claire countered with her own complaint. "And why did you storm off this afternoon?" Victor froze and simultaneously they recognized an impasse. Neither wanting to be pushed into uncomfortable territory, both desisted, retreating awkwardly into mundane topics. Surprisingly, these held intriguing veins of information. For instance, Claire discovered that Victor's mother Rose didn't know about their trip to Arkansas. "Dad never outright lied," he explained. "Just told her he wanted to spend the weekend with me. You know, let her think it was like always, at the lake."

Given his mother's obsessive control issues, Claire understood their need for such subterfuge and quickly turned the discussion to her news. "Mom says Glenn and Billy are becoming great chums. They visited the store together," she said, "and Billy was in great spirits."

Victor felt anxious. Twice in as many hours Billy had intruded on their conversation. "Maybe his father has finally left," he said.

"Maybe he just likes Glenn," she said, rolling onto her side.

Victor shook his head. "I don't think Billy likes anyone"— *except for you*. The thought darted so quickly behind his words that Victor feared he had spoken it aloud.

"What?" Claire sat up, intrigued.

Quickly standing, he strode to the door. "I want to catch the end of the game," he said, without looking back.

The next morning Victor sat moodily gazing out the vehicle window, where a simmering horizon lit an outline of the eastern sky. But as the fire of sunrise brightened, so did his mood until he sat eagerly staring out at the glossy expanse of Moon Lake. George pulled the SUV over soft ground, soggy from so much rain. He parked within a loose grove of overcup oak trees, receded from the shoreline. Tethered to a small tree nearer the bank, a long aluminum motorboat waited in the shallow water.

"Camouflage, cool," said Victor hurrying toward the mottled gray and green boat. Claire, however, stood right outside the vehicle, face uplifted to fragrant smells and tall oaks swelling with song. Hidden in high, leafy crowns were the singers: small, colorful birds of many different species. Tiny projectiles, they shot between branches and trees, visible only as streaking motion but audible everywhere. Whistling, trilling, buzzing—a sweet tempest of sound.

"What do you hear?" Robert said, pulling gear from the back of the SUV as George strolled toward his son by the bank. Claire's heart quickened. Was he testing her? She strained to pick out a particular song in the vocals swirling above and about her. At last a territorial call blared loud and insistent as a fire alarm.

Wik-wik-wik-wik-wik-wik-wik-wik-wik ...

"A noisy Northern Flicker, of course," she said, trying to sound casual. She drifted toward him.

"Yes, woodpeckers everywhere," Robert flashed his knowing smile, slinging a duffle back over his shoulder, "but never the Ivory-bill."

"I'll find him," she promised, back stepping awkwardly before him. "You'll see!"

Once outfitted with life vests stowed in the boat, Claire followed Robert into the hull, discouraged to see a smaller yet similar vessel, with two fishermen, motoring past. Their wake rolled beneath the boat causing her to loose balance as she stepped to the floor. Robert grabbed her underarm for support. Claire steadied herself before staggering toward one of two padded swivel chairs in the bow. Under the thick padding of her life vest, against the cotton of her woodpecker shirt, her heart pounded.

Victor boarded quickly, eager to claim the other chair beside Claire on the front fishing deck. Like a figurehead to the bow, she leaned stiffly forward, eyes and ears alert, seeming to pull the boat behind through sheer, intense will. Pointing ahead, she shouted, "Kingfisher!" All eyes sought the bird, diving bill first into the slate-gray water. With its plunge, everyone suspended their breath until the submerged bird thrust upward, flapping hard against the pull of water, a tiny fish gripped within the mandibles of its oversized crested head.

"Great catch, Claire!" George said, from his bench opposite Robert at the console. He pulled a small notepad from a pocket within his vest. "I'll keep a tally of all the birds we see or hear today."

The sun, cresting over the eastern tree line, sprayed golden light over the lake's western shore, where a long-bodied snake eased into the water. "Water Snake!" shouted Victor, like a game contestant before the buzzer sounds. Everyone followed his pointing hand.

"A Broad-banded Water Snake," affirmed his father. "Good catch, Victor."

Smiling broadly, Victor glanced to Claire, her eyes brimming with the snake's sinuous speed through the water. "It's not venomous," he added confidently, looking ahead. At reduced speed, the motorboat slipped into a narrowing channel, crowded on either side with large trees growing up from the muddy bayou, identified by Robert as baldcypress, a slow growing species that live hundreds of years. "In fact," he said, "there's one here in the refuge known as the Champion Tree estimated to be anywhere from 1000 to 1500 years old."

Victor whistled his astonishment.

"Hear that soft nasal *spee, spee, spee*?" Robert continued, looking directly to Claire. Try as she might, Claire couldn't detangle the sweet overgrowth of bird sounds. Cocking her head like Robert, squeezing her eyes, she strained to hear.

"I hear it!" announced Victor. "It's that soft, scratchy sound." He turned to Claire with grinning eyes that taunted her. "Can't you hear it?" She slid a scorching glare his way before lifting an opposite ear to the sky.

"Spee, spee, spee—There it goes again," Robert said while Claire exhaled in futility. Why couldn't she hear it? Mercifully, Victor's father ended her torment. "A Blue-gray Gnatcatcher, I think," he said, winking to his son.

For moments Claire lost all confidence in her ears, now strangely deaf to birdsong but for a throbbing, shrill monotone

161

of their collective voices. She tugged at her life jacket and pumped it against her chest in the muggy, warm morning. Face upturned, she surveyed the tree canopy under which they slid, a vaulted green tunnel spackled with sunlight and a central swath of blue sky. She imagined the fabled red-crested bird pumping its black and white wings toward her. Victor meanwhile attended the muddy water and bank, whose denizens seemed eager to be counted. Repeatedly, he shouted sightings of bullfrogs, turtles, more water snakes, even large fish breaking the surface.

I wish he'd just shut up, she thought, increasingly anxious that his noise would scare away the Ivory-bill.

"Another bullfrog!"

Shut up! Shut up! Shut up! She shouted to him mentally. Why did they blather on so? Was no one serious about sighting the Ivory-bill? Pulsing blood echoed in her eardrums. She could hear and feel nothing but her body—perspiring temples and itchy, sweaty palms. She pulled the stupid cap from her damp head, opening to sight the skyline. A large, dark bird flew above the trees over the bayou. It headed directly toward them. Each upstroke of the bird's wings flashed white.

Claire clutched the binoculars about her neck. Eyes on target, arms suddenly heavy, she raised them to position. Her fingertip skidded over the focus knob, producing a blur. She groaned. In an instant the winged mystery would disappear. With naked eyes she sought the bird, unaltered in its flight path. Binoculars again positioned, she dialed into focus a blazing red crest. The color swelled within her pupils like an optic supernova. She catapulted from her seat, arm rigidly pointing: "Ivory-bill!"

In her mind's eye, Claire could see Victor's father stand to hoist the camera. She could hear the boat's motor sputter to a stop, could feel time suspend while each directed his senses to the woodpecker pulling upward with deeply rowing wings, banking toward the canopy of cypress, disappearing into a cloud of green needles. Gone.

In motionless expectation, everyone awaited Robert's confirmation. But his deep sigh foretold a disappointing proclamation. "Pileated."

A wave of red, hot shame flooded Claire's face and she collapsed, sack like, onto the chair.

Starting the motor, Robert attempted to ease her dejection. "Good practice, even so." Then opening the throttle full tilt, he shouted over the engine. "Today was just a drill. We won't find an Ivory-bill here."

18

The Champion Tree

From Moon Lake, they traveled a few miles southeast on Highway 1, turning south on to a more rural road. Claire stared through her sealed window at deep fields of green rice. She felt bitterly betrayed by Robert. Had he told her the outing to Moon Lake was to be a "drill," she never would have worn the Ivory-bill shirt. But she did wear it and so faced a distressing unknown: what would happen if the day passed without her seeing or hearing the elusive woodpecker? Never had she not seen the bird displayed on her shirt.

Heedless of Claire's worries, Victor grilled Robert for more details on their next destination, the Champion Tree. "How big is it?" he asked, perched sideways on the edge of the back seat.

"About eleven foot in diameter and 150 feet high."

Victor whistled. Soon he would look upon a tree seen by native peoples hundreds of years before Europeans ever dreamed of a New World. Seeing it would be like traveling back in time. A sudden worry creased his brow. "It isn't surrounded by some stupid parking lot?"

Robert chuckled, pulling a refuge map from the glove compartment. He unfolded the map, extending it between the seats. "Look," he pointed with an immaculately manicured finger. "We enter the refuge here. Drive a mile or so over a gravel road and then hike in for another mile."

Claire restrained herself from looking, preferring to mope. Arms clamped across chest, she gazed out over the monotonous fields and said, sullenly, "I don't even see a forest." Victor tried to show Claire the tree's location on the map but she slapped it away. "Why aren't we searching for the Ivory-bill?" she whined, opening the window to a warm, onrushing current.

From Ethel, a hamlet two miles west of the refuge border, they drove over narrow country roads to Refuge Road, a macadam-covered rut. Through an expanse of open prairie, it led to the forest. Within the tree-shaded but humid refuge, they crawled over a gravel road, tires skidding in the deep grade of stones. Claire and Victor plunged their noses into an earthy stew of smells—of green leaves and tree bark, of dark soil and oozing mud, of stagnant water and gentle floral scents. Raining throughout was sunshine, golden shafts teeming with wisps of flying life, and everywhere the music of birds.

Eventually they crossed a car-width bridge over a narrow bayou brimming with muddy water that threatened to overflow the planks thumping beneath their tires. They followed the winding road that dipped sharply, leading them deeper yet into the refuge. Moments later they pulled into a small clearing, where a Red-headed Woodpecker perched atop a wooden signpost marking the trail.

Victor shouted, "Is that a Red-headed Woodpecker?"

Disappointed not to have seen it first, Claire snidely asked, "What gave it away? Its red head?" As the woodpecker flew off, both backseat occupants bolted from the SUV, at once shrieking against an onslaught of mosquitoes. Robert stood armed with a can of repellent to spray everyone's wrists and ankles. They packed water and trail mix for provisions and headed out on the short mile-long hike.

Claire and Victor sprinted ahead on the wide path through the hardwoods. But the hot, heavy air clogging their lungs soon slowed them to a brisk walk. With the adults safely distant, Victor grabbed Claire by the upper arm. "What's wrong with you?" he said. "You've been acting like a super jerk." She pulled away as they broke to circle a large pool flooding the path, he on one side, she the other.

Arms outstretched for balance while walking a log, Claire said, "What do you think?"

"I think trying to impress your boyfriend is making you batty," he said, wearing a superior smirk.

They quickened their pace to keep distant from the adults, only to be repeatedly slowed by small pools obliterating the path. Each they circumvented with resolve, except when distracted by some lizard-like newt, salamander, or frog.
In fact, preoccupied as they were anticipating the next water hurdle, they would have stomped right past the Champion Tree but not for a canal. Many feet wide and several deep, it

barred their way like a castle mote. From its standing water, a pair of wood ducks flushed. Wings thrashing air, the ducks rose at a diagonal, crossing the towering cypress. Only then did the startled hikers see the tree: a mighty, muscled Goliath of wood and bark, a sentinel against time.

Among a host of younger cypress the Champion stood supreme, in girth nearly 35 feet—so large it appeared to occupy rather than grow from the ground. Their eyes climbed the massive trunk creased with bulging folds of age. Rooted in a past millennium, the Champion had withstood the plunder of time and man.

"This tree is sacred," Victor said, eyes lifting ever upward.

Claire felt it, too, like she should bow or genuflect.

"Do you know why it's so ancient?" he asked, head titling in that way characteristic of his father, gaze steady and serious.

Thinking, she looked up into the scattered, tiered clouds of cypress needles. "Well, it didn't die from disease, so it must be strong." She stepped closer to the bank, hands to hips, and over a shoulder added, "And no tornado ever brought it down, so it must be lucky."

Victor stepped beside her, their shoulders touching. "Tahwach," he said, intimately, "this tree is more than lucky." He waited for her shielded eyes to rest on his. "At some point, loggers took all the other trees." He waved an arm across the scene. "See how much younger they are. So why didn't loggers take the Champion?"

Lifting soft, snowy brows, she smiled. "I don't know."

He watched her coyly, dark eyes gleaming. "I think this tree is special to Mother Earth. I think she protects it."

Like a butterfly the idea fluttered in time to her blinking eyelids. His sweet, sincerely stated belief surprised and then captivated her. She looked to him and then the tree. "I never would have thought that," she said quietly.

"Tahwach, the Earth is alive, just like you and me. Mother Earth talks to us through all living things. She especially talks to you."

Claire jerked her head his way, face lit expectantly. "She talks to me?"

He grinned, tempted to tease her. "Your birds," he said. "*They* talk to you."

Any other time, Claire would have felt proud about her connection to birds but not now. Her disappointment confused him, but he pressed on. "Every person has an animal guide that walks with him or her through life. Mine is the black bear. And that's why my father gave me the black bear's name—*Muh'nah'kain Kuhaia*." He felt a sudden urge to chastise her for never using his native name.

"What do animal guides do?" Doubt colored her tone as she stepped back to survey the area. "And how did your father know that yours was a black bear?"

He followed her to a bench behind them neither had earlier noted. They sat down. "An animal guide leads you where you're going, whether on a hike through the woods or to join this or that club in school."

"And your animal is a bear?"

He nodded.

"But how do you know?"

He told the story his father had told him many times. How the morning his mother awoke to labor pains, a big black bear peered in through the bedroom window. "But more incredibly," he said, "when they got back with me the next day, that same bear waited for them on our front stoop!"

"You're kidding!" she cried, excited yet suspicious of the story.

"My dad knew right then—the black bear was my guide, so he marched with me in his arms toward the front door and that bear jumped from the porch and just lumbered off." Victor enjoyed tantalizing Claire. "And I know your animal guide. Dad told me."

Claire's eyes blazed with interest, but Victor paused, straining to listen through the bird chatter for sound of the approaching adults. Detecting nothing, he continued.

"The Red-tailed Hawk."

"You mean Ku-Khain?" she said, voice shrill with expectancy.

"Not exactly. The animal guide is spirit and can go everywhere with you." Seeing Claire's disappointment, he hurried to explain. "But Ku-Khain is spirit, too. So are we."

He tapped his chest. "Everyone alive is mostly spirit, just temporarily clothed in flesh."

Claire always expected to become spirit when she died but to be one while still alive was an exhilarating idea. She sprang from the bench. "So is Ku-Khain my guide or not?"

"I thought I was your guide," said Robert, bouncing onto the scene, wearing a cheeky grin. Neither had heard his approach and both stiffened in surprise. Victor stood abruptly and Claire turned awkwardly from the intruder. Robert had not heard the conversation, only Claire's last remark. However, seeing their avoidance he did not press for an answer but motioned them to the tree for a photo.

Hours later, exhausted from heat and additional sightseeing, all welcomed the air-conditioned drive back north. And none were eager to leave the cool confines of the SUV when finally George pulled into the crowded parking lot of the Community Store and Restaurant, known for its weekly catfish buffet and crawfish boil. A long, squat building, it sat on Arkansas Highway 1, about a mile east of the refuge visitor center and at an intersection leading into the town of St. Charles. Outside the vehicle, Robert winked to George from across a blazing hood. "I hope you kids like mudbugs," he said to the pair, each squinting against the sun. "Because that's what we're having for dinner."

The young allies stood horrified and then confused. "Come on," George said laughing as he mussed his son's hair, and they headed up onto the cement porch and through a screen door. Inside, warm air from high pedestal fans blew against their faces and spicy scents of Cajun cooking seeped into their nostrils.

Oak and glass display cases divided the expansive room into two areas, the store portion at the front, lined with plate glass windows, and the larger restaurant behind. People sat there laughing and talking, bent over tables covered with newspaper and heaped with orange-shelled crawfish. Past displays of stuffed ducks, duck lures, and fishing hats, the group shuffled toward the maze of crowded tables. Looking for empty seats, they surveyed the scene, while those seated surveyed them, pausing, Claire thought, too long on her, a ghost-colored stranger among sun-baked folk. Far back, on the right, someone stood to motion them in—it was Zondra.

"Hey!" Claire cried, excited to see a familiar face.
Expertly she navigated the sea of diners, squeezing through crowded chairs, once stumbling over an extraneous limb.

Dressed in her khaki uniform, Zondra greeted them. "Got off from work and thought to save you a table." She directed a smile to each, reserving its radiance at last for Robert. His intense, anxious eyes groped for hers.

Claire would not order the crawfish boil, nor could she be coaxed to take even one bite of the flesh of the small, lobster-like crustacean. The litter of its shells and body parts soaking the newsprint made her too nauseous even to eat her grilled cheese and fries. Instead she sipped on a cold soda while watching Robert and Zondra directly opposite. Chasing her every glance, he nodded in agreement to whatever she said, his face possessed of a silly grin. In fact, Robert acted so stupidly that it fell to Victor's father to direct a sensible conversation, one with an exchange of information. Thus they learned that though Zondra grew up in Little Rock, with three younger brothers, she was no stranger to the refuge.

"Our father brought us here every year for vacation," she said smiling with the memory. "And each time we'd explore some place new. It was a child's paradise! Trotline fishing for catfish, hunting for crawfish—" she abruptly stopped to direct a question to her younger listeners. "Did you know that crawfish build mud chimneys on stream banks many feet underwater?"

Neither knew this and indicated likewise.

"But can you think of why they do it?"

Here Robert interrupted, intent on drawing back Zondra's attention. "I know! I know," he said, raising a hand, pretending to be a know-it-all. (Never did he suspect the others to see his true character in this charade.)

Victor leaned against Claire's shoulder to whisper with greasy crawfish lips into her ear. "Looks like your boyfriend already has a girl." In response, she shoved him hard with her shoulder and from the pile of crawfish grabbed a small corncob to fling at him.

19

Double Knocks

On the road after dinner, Robert at last disclosed where they would camp for the night: Hickson Lake on Dagmar Wildlife Management Area. In the fading day, they drove north for an hour until reaching the woodland. In the deepened dusk of tree cover, George switched on the headlights to a sudden flurry of pale moths. The humid evening air, throbbing with the sound of crickets, smelled sweet. Roused from fatigue, Claire and Victor sat upright, watching expectantly out the windows.

The winding, gravel road took them past a few unoccupied primitive campsites, clearings large enough for a camper or tent. Everyone could smell the water though none could see it through the ever-darkening woods. Within these trees shone a soft amber light winking to them from behind each passing trunk.

"Is that it?" Claire clutched Robert's headrest to pull forward.

"That's it," he said. "Tonight we camp in style."

Crunching gravel the tires rolled toward a final bend in the road behind which stood a large, illuminated tent. Victor spilled from the backdoor, Claire instantly beside him. Toward and through the open flaps of the canvas dwelling they hurried, Victor crying, "A safari tent!"

Chapter 19

Once again the billionaire's assistants had prepared their accommodations, including a fire ring with tinder and logs for lighting. With renewed energy the group unpacked the vehicle and then started a fire, eager to enjoy the evening. Thereafter Claire and Victor drifted lakeside, the fire bright behind them, its wood smoke a gentle perfume to the air. Through the darkness they strained to see the far shore. "Doesn't it seem ages ago since we were at the School House Lodge?" said Claire.

Victor wrinkled his nose in a grin. "It does, Tahwach."

They stood on a paved boat launch inches from the water, black as oil under a moonless sky. Even without moonlight, Claire's white hair glowed with stray light from the not too distant blaze. He stared solemnly into her face. She couldn't read his expression in the dark but sensed a mood change.

"Why don't you ever call me *Muh'nah'kain Kuhaia*?"

Claire sighed heavily. "Because it's hard to pronounce." She waited for a reaction, scuffing the ground with her foot. "Besides, I can't call you that when other people are around, so I forget when we're alone."

Victor wasn't convinced. "For months you asked me to tell you my Indian name." A deep breath foretold the severity of his coming criticism. "So how do you think I feel now that you refuse to use it?"

The hurt in his voice made her defensive. "Well how do you think I feel when you don't even care if I see the Ivory-billed Woodpecker?"

174

Victor nearly snorted. "Excuse me, Claire." He dropped her name like a heavy load. "I forgot. Everything always has to be about you." He turned and stomped away.

Claire and Victor's argument bled the joy from their safari tent experience. Within the white cocoons of their respective netting, they both brooded, listening to the insistent buzzing of blood-sucking mosquitoes. Well before dawn, they rose in twilight to that strangely quiet time that follows the night music of crickets and anticipates the morning choir of birds. Taking only the ice chests of food and drinks, they hurriedly left camp en route to Bayou DeView.

Sharing a moody silence in the back seat, Claire and Victor devoured their breakfast hoagies that filled the interior with the strong odor of raw onions. Thirty minutes later, several miles northeast of camp, they turned off Route 17 to a boat launch below the road. As on Moon Lake, their transport awaited: two stocked canoes rested on the rutted, muddy bank, where a dead fish fouled the air with the stench of decay. Annoyed, Robert scooped up the bloated corpse with a canoe paddle. "They could have taken care of this," he said of his never-seen assistants, and flung it into the dense vegetation above the bank.

Victor found Crowley's scowl an improvement over his fake smiles but didn't care for Claire's continued glum mood. Even now she kept apart, standing far behind them by the vehicle. Bent over a canoe, Robert demonstrated to Victor's father an electric motor powered by a car battery, explaining that it made less noise then paddling. Though interested in this "trolling" motor, Victor dashed up the sloping dirt lane to Claire. "Don't be upset, Tawach," he said, poking her in the sides to make her jump, which she did, grinning despite herself. She wanted to say his Indian name but was afraid to mispronounce it. "Say it for me," she said.

He knew her meaning, saying, "Repeat after me," and led her through the syllables until at last she spoke his name with some confidence. "Muh'nah'kain Kuhaia."

He grinned, pushing up his cap visor. "Was that so hard?" Yanking the cap down his nose, she expertly dodged his groping hands, racing him to the canoes. There he petitioned his father to let him share one with Claire but was rejected. "One adult per canoe," George said. "You with me; Claire with Robert."

"At least let me steer," he rejoined, expecting some consolation but receiving none. Crouching, he shuffled in heavy Muck boots to the front of the wobbling boat. George pushed the canoe into the milky, muddy water, launching it as he jumped onboard. Claire and Robert replayed this scene with their own canoe until all were "trolling" southward with the slow-moving current.

They floated on the misty, quiet waters through a corridor of cypress and tupelo whose bloated bases looked like gargantuan toads. Beyond these stood an entire regiment of amphibious swamp trees. Once a numberless host, their dense ranks were in fact sadly shallow, perhaps a mile in width. Yet imbuing the forest was a primal power derived from all that lived within. In the meager light of dawn, the travelers glided reverently through the gray-green trunks.

The sky steadily brightened above the lofty, mingling trees, whose crowns held the morning bustle and chatter of warblers and gnatcatchers. And the Blue-gray's soft, nasal call (*spee spee spee*) that had so eluded Claire on Indian Bayou now whispered through the morning air directly into her ear. It seemed to say, "*This is it! This is it! This is it!*"

This is the day you find the Ivory-bill.

Coasting with the sluggish current, the two-canoe expedition weaved among the trees increasingly crowding the channel. To the thrill of the forward-seated watch, they glided past many Diamond-back Water Snakes coiled or stretched in luxurious length along bare, brittle branches or fallen trunks.

"Number one rule," Robert proclaimed while steering the lead canoe through an especially tight passage between two mighty cypresses, "always watch your back." He nodded to his right and a shelf in the cypress trunk, at head level, on which two massive Cottonmouths lay coiled together mating.

Seconds earlier, Claire had passed unknowingly within feet of the snakes whose heads were now upright, alert, and swaying.

"Dad, what should I do?" Victor asked, gripped in anxiety. "Should I duck?"

Chapter 19

Already too far into the passage to back out, George spoke calmly. "No sudden moves, son. Just relax. They'll let us pass." Chest contracting in a silent sigh, Victor closed his eyes tightly, face gripped in tension. He wondered if snakes, like dogs, could sense fear. His heart skipped when the canoe scraped the tree base. Then his father was saying, "We're by now. See? No big deal."

When sunlight gilding the treetops began washing through their crowns, Claire asked Robert when they would reach the spot of David Luneau's famous and only recent video of the Ivory-billed Woodpecker. Her faith had not diminished, yet she needed a confidence booster.

"Not far now," he assured her. "But let's first 'knock' to see if anyone's home." The oddity of this remark had its intended effect. Claire twisted in her seat to look back again at Robert, and George cut his motor to keep from trolling past the lead canoe. Everyone waited for an explanation, which Robert withheld, as typical, for the sake of suspense. He backed the canoe, motor first, to a swell of soggy ground surrounding a smaller cypress. The channel extended as a shallow pool deep into the hardwoods beyond. Digging his paddle into the muck, he nudged the stern up onto the soft ground crowded with gnarly, gray cypress knees.

"You guys stay inside the canoe," he instructed while climbing out into foot-high water and soft sediments that instantly cemented his feet. He tugged one foot and then the other but neither budged. In dismay, he shook his head of dark curls, clumped in sweat, and reached a hand behind. "Could you get me a paddle?"

Claire grinned with the others, hunching her shoulders in playful, non-verbal comment. "Sure!" She crept on deep-bended knees down the canoe to grab and hoist a paddle toward his waiting hand. Using it for balance, Robert tugged and tugged until the muck relented with a loud sucking pop and splash of water. One appendage free, he probed the ground with the paddle, searching for a more solid foothold. Finding one, he stepped to that spot to try to pull his back foot out. Another sucking pop and he fell forward, between two craggy cypress knees, arms braced to break the fall.

"Oh-h-h-h!" his spectators cried as Robert crawled to a stooping stance, his lap soaked with water, mud splattered across his life vest. He stood, turned, and hoisted a paddle in victory, while everyone laughed and clapped.

"Don't laugh too hard," he said in good-natured jest, dropping the paddle to wipe gritty, wet hands against his camouflaged pants. "The day's just begun and the swamp will demand its due." He winked at Victor who, surprising himself, returned an earnest smile.

Quickly back to business, Robert hauled more of the canoe onto the ground. Beneath the stern deck he removed a wooden device called a 'double knocker,' designed, as he explained, to mimic the Ivory-billed Woodpecker's unique drumming. "Since the Ivory-bill is an endangered species," he said, hoisting the devise upward for all to see, "it's illegal to harass the woodpecker by imitating its sounds unless you get a permit from the US Fish & Wildlife Service." Patting his chest pocket, he indicated that such a permit resided within.

The double knocker had two parts: a box-like base for striking (which he strapped against the tree trunk with rope) and a striker: two thick, wooden dowels hinged to a large bolt to swing independent, but in sequence, of the other. Grabbing its wooden grip, he struck the base hard producing two loud, successive knocks that reverberated through the forest.

"If another Ivory-bill is within hearing distance, he should respond." Robert again struck the base: **KNOCK**-knock. Everyone listened attentively to the sound traveling through the stand of stoic gray-trunked trees. Claire imagined an Ivory-bill, somewhere within hearing distance, turning its head toward the sound. She knew he was out there, knew it to her core. Again Robert struck the base: **KNOCK**-knock. Claire's vague mental image of the red-crested male became vivid, sharp. Closing her eyes she saw it as on a screen—no, more three dimensional. She saw the male launch from a high limb in a towering cypress and fly to an adjacent tupelo. He cocked his head to listen as Robert struck the base. **KNOCK**-knock.

In response, the woodpecker in Claire's mind pounded the tupelo with his bone-hard bill: **KNOCK**-knock.

"Did you hear that?" she asked urgently.

"What?" Victor sat only feet away, behind and a bit downstream of Claire.

"An ivory-bill rapping!"

Everyone tilted their heads, ears cocked to the air, listening. Only the sweet ramblings of songbirds and the distant drumming of a Pileated Woodpecker could be heard.

"Hit it again," she ordered. Robert immediately obliged.

KNOCK-knock.

Again Claire saw a mental image of the Ivory-bill cocking his head to listen. And again the bird vigorously responded:

KNOCK-knock.

"Surely you heard it that time?" she said, a plea to her voice.

"You don't mean that Pileated, do you?" Robert asked.

"No!" she shouted, a fresh burn of shame from yesterday's mistaken identification coloring her face. "Twice I heard a double-knock—just like you're making!"

Victor's father attempted to calm her. "Your hearing must be better than ours, Claire." He back-paddled to draw alongside her. "Try again, Robert, and this time we'll all bend our ears to it."

Once again Robert struck the base but this time Claire neither saw the Ivory-bill in her mind nor heard it respond.

"It's gone!" she said in an icy tone to imply their wrongdoing. Given her mood, no one challenged the insinuation that somehow they were at fault. Instead, Robert climbed into the canoe to resume the trip downstream.

20

The Ivory-billed Woodpecker

Claire couldn't tell whether she'd seen the woodpecker in her mind or with her eyes. And what of his loud knocking? Yet the others didn't hear it. Could her hearing be *that* superior? Lost in this analysis, she took little note of the surroundings, finding it difficult even to express enthusiasm when finally they arrived to the site of David Luneau's video.

"On April 25, 2004," Robert said, cutting the motor and grabbing a paddle, "University of Arkansas professor David Luneau and his brother-in-law, Robert Henderson, captured on video eleven wing beats of the Ivory-billed Woodpecker." Robert maneuvered the canoe to face upstream among a press of bottom-heavy trees, shaded in hues of emerald moss or charcoal, a sign of extended water submersion. "I'm going to recreate that sighting," he said, coaching Claire to sit facing into the canoe and positioned to his left, exactly as Henderson. Everywhere over the milky surface, like a living veneer, skittered water beetles. "George, move your canoe here beside ours."

Oddly detached from the moment, Claire ignored a persistent birdsong and with slumped shoulders watched George draw alongside. Victor arranged himself as Claire but avoided eye contact, annoyed with her volatile mood swings. The trees began to creak and whine with a light wind, a contrast to the cheery voice of the songster: *zee-zee-zee, zee-zee-zee.*

"What's that bird?" Victor asked, squinting into the canopy overhead.

"That is the Prothonotary Warbler, a sweet yellow bird as at home in these swamps as was the Ivory-bill." Robert looked expectantly to Claire. "Another bird for your Life List, Claire?"

Returning a blank expression, she nodded.

"Okay, then!" Robert clapped his hands. "Imagine the scene with me. The Ivory-bill flew from the base of a water tupelo about 20 meters from where we sit." He pointed left into the ranks of gray tree trunks, lustrously mottled with noonday sun. "Luneau's video caught four seconds of a large black and white woodpecker flying off on a slightly inclining trajectory through those trees."

Peering into the canopies of tupelo and cypress swaying with a welcomed breeze, Victor said, "One could be in the trees watching us right now." He saw the re-enactment as a ceremony to honor the woodpecker. Claire, however, saw it as a distraction from what she suddenly realized to be true: the woodpecker would come to her and her alone. The others served only to ward off her secretive bird.

"I'm hungry," she said, yanking all from reverie, and then asked, "Are we ever going to eat?"

On her insistent note, they commenced travel downstream

through a dense huddle of swampland trees often nearly blocking their passage. Robert and Claire maneuvered the canoe through resolute ranks, where no visible channel held sway, where the ground or submerged trunk might collide with their hulls. Against each new obstruction they prodded or pushed with their paddles, while George and Victor scouted a different route. Temples trickling with sweat, skin sticking to her shirt, Claire mutinied. "It's too hot to wear this stupid life jacket," she whined, unclasping and throwing it behind her into the hull.

"Fair enough," said George turning to face her. He and Victor now led the way, having avoided the snares. "But you'll need to put it back on once we reach the lake." Claire agreed though not intending to honor that contract, because to attract the Ivory-bill she must do two things: 1) expose her shirt front with his image and 2) separate herself from the others. How to manage the latter, she didn't yet know.

The trees, gradually parting, formed an aisle through which the canoes floated unhindered. As the channel widened so did the slice of sky above, crowded with pearly, luminous clouds behind which the sun took repeated cover. The deepening water acquired a steely cast and quickly carried them from among the trees out onto a large, long lake.

"This is Stab Lake," announced Robert proudly. "And I know a special high spot where we can eat lunch, that is, if the bugs don't eat us first." A quenching breeze rippled the surface water, and all inhaled deeply of the cold, fresh depths rolling beneath.

Under an enormous sky, George said, "Good deal—but what about chiggers?" Being a man of the outdoors, he knew all about these larvae of mites that inhabit damp, warm vegetative areas. In such places, only fools would sit on the ground since nothing is more inviting to a chigger than a warm human bottom. Robert, however, assured him of the safety and comfort to be found in his completely enclosed pop-up picnic shelter.

George cast a gaze eastward, above a towering line of baldcypress. "Is that an Anhinga flying there?" The large, cormorant-like water bird, black against a bank of clouds, flapped and glided his way northward, providing all ample time for study through binoculars.

"That it is," said Robert.

An electric fizz flashed over Claire's skin, jump-starting her torpid senses. The Anhinga carried a message for her in the beat of its silver-dusted wings! She didn't understand the meaning but felt the message pulsing in her blood. Exhilarated, she looked back to Robert, entreaty in her shielded eyes cast gray-green with the water. Maybe he could interpret the message carried by the Anhinga, the one still singing in her veins? Robert winked at Claire, marveling at her hair, white as any of the cumulus clouds sailing overhead.

Guiding their canoes due east, they trolled at full speed

toward the tree line over which the Anhinga had flown. To reach the "high spot" hidden just inside the woodland, they needed to traverse only the width of the lake, not its length, which well suited Claire. She felt too jittery for further confinement in the canoe. They began crossing the wide expanse with sunshine splashing over the lake. But persistent clouds chased and scattered the sparkling trails, so that when they reached the hulky, water-wise hardwoods, the last blaze was extinguished.

"Cut your motor," called Robert. "We're going to paddle just inside these trees." Over shallow water they slid among trunks suggestive of elephant hide toward a tiny island the size of a large room. A grove of trees, neither cypress nor tupelo, held ground against the mightier force surrounding them.

"What species of tree is this?" asked George, banking his canoe alongside Robert. Both men stepped into foot-high water to drag their boats farther up the bank.

"Overcup oak," he grunted while tugging the canoe. "Like those we saw at Moon Lake." Claire shuffled forward in the canoe but then stopped, seeming to attend to Robert's explanation. "Even small undulations of the topography are enough to alter species composition," he said, stepping up to an oak.

Scrambling out of his canoe, Victor didn't notice Claire's hesitation or what had caught her attention: another island of land. Shaped like a finger, its far end was not visible while its near shore lay only 50 feet behind the land on which they banked. Claire saw this as her opportunity to separate from the others. In a tone of exaggerated complaint, she said, "I need to relieve myself."

Robert and George exchanged looks to see who would respond. Then Victor added, "So do I."

George cleared his throat, putting hands to hips. "We all do, I suspect," he said, heavily exhaling. Turning in a circle he scanned the layout. "Claire, what if you go to the far end behind those trees, and we men will go right off to this side."

"No."

The men stopped, silent and awkward.

"Okay, Claire," George said calmly. "What's your plan?"

"This island is too small. I need privacy. Why can't I go to that ground over there?" She pointed to the finger of land where the oaks swayed with a rush of wind. Somewhat confounded, Robert and George again exchanged looks.

"Well . . . " Robert headed toward the canoe. "I guess I can paddle you over—"

"No!" Claire grabbed one of the paddles. "I can paddle myself."

"No you don't," Robert said, looking obstinate as any parent. "You're not paddling yourself."

"I am too!" she shrieked, climbing over the gunwale into the water to shove the canoe free.

Robert rushed to grab the stern. "What are you doing?" Baffled, he looked back to the others. None could understand her bizarre behavior. Both adults goaded Victor with their eyes to intervene. He rushed toward the canoe.

"Claire, you're acting crazy!" he said. "Stop tugging at the canoe." Instantly she relented. Seeming irrational would not help her cause.

Everyone sighed and relaxed a bit, waiting for the other to speak. As the only female, Claire understood her advantage.

"I have to go!" she whined, linking her strange behavior to a biological urgency. "For Heaven's sake, I know how to paddle a canoe. And I'm only going over there." She pointed to the short distance. "I won't even be out of sight."

The males could not deny her need for relief or privacy and so conceded. Claire climbed back into the canoe, water trailing into the hull from her Muck boots, and Victor shoved it free of the bank. "We'll just watch until you get there."

"But don't dawdle," George warned. "The wind is picking up and I think a storm is coming. In fact," he turned to Robert, "it might be best to ride it out here."

"No problem. Let's pop up that tent and get the food out."

As it turned out the food chests were with Claire, urgently paddling toward the other island and her rendezvous with the Ivory-bill. "Come quickly," she said softly to the woodpecker held in her mind. "We don't have much time." She heard the others crowding the remaining canoe to haul out the pop-up tent, preparing to erect it against a coming storm. She tried waving away a maddening cloud of gnats attracted to her sweaty brow, but each time it reassembled. Her only relief, the repellent-treated cap, lay uselessly near the bow.

"I have to get my cap," she cried for the benefit of the others who might be watching.

"Don't try it!" Robert called back, his curls tossing with a persistent wind.

"I have to!" she hollered, knowing they couldn't stop her, and scooted off the seat. She slid on her bottom to the stern thwart, or cross strut, onto which Robert had attached a tripod with zip ties for the mounted video camera, in handy reach of the person steering. Both canoes had cameras running the entire time, a trick Robert learned from Luneau. These were aimed a little to one side to avoid the heads of the persons sitting in the bow. As Robert had explained, "Since no one knows where the woodpecker is going to appear, aiming the camera to one spot is as good as another."

Climbing over the cross strut crowded with equipment would be tricky, so she moved slowly, despite gnats diving at her eyes. Once over, she slid again on her bottom to the midship thwart. Instead of crawling over, she slid her long legs beneath, reaching for the cap with her foot. Anchoring it beneath a heavy heel, she pulled it back.

"Got it!" She waved the cap in the air before tugging it low to her forehead.

"Paddle from right there," George urged. "Don't go back to your seat." She waved an affirmative to which he congenially responded. "And hurry. You got the food and we're starving."

Claire paddled toward the raised ground, mindful of the video camera at her back. With no one looking, she must remove it from the mount to carry with her. "I'm here!" she shouted, climbing over the gunwale to pull the canoe onto the soggy bank. "Now don't look!"

Waving acknowledgements, the men dutifully turned away to pursue their activities and Claire leaned into the canoe to slip the camera free of its mount. Earlier Robert had demonstrated the process. Camera held against her stomach, she waded through the water, deep muck sucking her soles. On land she stumbled ahead, frantic to get out of view. A surprisingly strong gust pushed her along through the loose grove of oak whose leaves trembled high overhead.

Claire's full bladder was not a pretense, and at first opportunity she relieved herself behind a large tree. The ground beyond her did not end abruptly, as she had expected, but narrowed to a mere winding walkway through the flooded bottomland. She would follow it but needed more time. Darting from behind the tree, she took several paces toward the canoe and hollered into the wind, "I can't find a good place."

"What?" called Victor's father.

"I can't find a good place," she bellowed.

"Go anywhere," he called, gaze averted from the adjacent island. "No one's watching."

In a shrill, plaintive tone intended to intimidate, she cried, "Give me some time!" and bolted toward the land bridge, a leaf-sodden spine that surely would lead to the waiting Ivory-bill. With barely minutes to find and record the woodpecker, Claire tried to calm herself despite a heart keeping double-time. Inches above water, the walkway cut through a small open area that led to a group of tupelo. With no time to marvel or speculate, she strained to see an endpoint through the gray trunks and water.

While Robert and George struggled to erect the shelter against a rising wind, Victor was sent to retrieve seat cushions from the canoe. He envied Claire her opportunity to explore but dared not look in that direction. Instead he stared through the trees over the restless lake frothing at the shore. Foamy white water lapped his boots where earlier footprints were dry. He tugged the canoe farther up onto the bank.

Since calling out, Claire gauged a minute had passed. Hastily crossing the land bridge, she stumbled, almost falling into a deep waterhole. Her heart froze like the spring of a tightly wound toy. Through a crop of gnarly cypress knees sprouting from the water, she plodded toward a lone cypress on a mound of earth. Turning her back to its ragged trunk, she slid downward, eager to sit, until remembering—"Chiggers!" She pushed back upward brooding over the hostility of a place where you couldn't sit on the ground. How she longed for her own woodlands and her beloved Sammy! His absence burned

191

her eyes.

Meanwhile, Victor stared wonderingly at an upheaval of cumulous mountains in the sky everywhere pierced by a fierce sun. Radiance strained toward the lake but could not reach it. The brooding waters, agitated by a southwest wind, were choppy and irritable. Victor inhaled these forces and felt himself invigorated. Crawling into the canoe, he glanced again out over the lake, where a distant bird flew from the southwest, heading eastward to their shore. Careful not to rock the boat, he rose from a crouched posture to watch. The dark bird, a duck he suspected, flew high through dispersed strains of golden light coating his plumage with a stellar sheen. For a better view, he raised the binoculars.

"Is Claire heading back?" George called to his son, who needed a moment more to spy on the duck.

"I'll check," he cried, focusing the lens that instantly exposed his error. The bird was not a duck; it was a woodpecker.

"Whoa!" His lungs emptied with the word, because the bird's red crest was well receded from the forehead. Flying toward him was an Ivory-billed Woodpecker. Victor gulped air and screamed, "Claire!"

Claire heard Victor's call. "No," she moaned, resenting his intrusion. "I need time." Obstinately she sank downward against the trunk, forgetting entirely of chiggers.

"Claire!" Victor cried with an intensity that brought both men running down to the bank.

"What?" demanded his father, frantic for some sign of the girl. Victor only pointed to the sky.

George was first to lock his gaze on the bird, only two hundred feet away. "Good Lord," he uttered.

"It can't be," said Robert, straining naked eyes to discern if the pumping wings trailed with white edging.

"Victor, the video!" his father called. "Get it! Quickly!"

Victor dropped to his knees over the strut holding the mount. He prayed that the camera would slip easily from its lock and it did.

"Film it!" shrieked Robert, binocular vision revealing the fabled bird's clown-like face. "Film it!" His was a desperate, raging plea.

Victor fumbled the camera, nearly dropping it. Hands trembling, he hoisted it upward to the bird. In the video finder, the woodpecker looked more distant, yet he could see the male's striking, even comical, face—glossy black with a flaming red crest; button eyes with bright yellow irises; a snaking white stripe climbing from his back, up his neck, and ending beneath the eye; an enormous ivory bill.

"Are you getting it?" cried Robert, unable to break vision with the bird.

But Victor did not answer. Already suffering his friend's loss, he whispered mournfully, "Tawach." For here, within his gaze, flew the bird most sought and revered in recent history . . . but where was Claire?

The woodpecker flew overhead his amazed spectators and into the forest—heading directly toward the adjacent island.

"Claire!" Victor's call held a suddenly hopeful tone.

Three times assailed by Victor's outcries, Claire stubbornly clutched her knees, hugging them to her chest. Already they were calling her back. But she didn't care and wouldn't leave without seeing her woodpecker. Raising a pitiful face, she wailed with the boughs groaning in the wind. "Where are you?"

A gusting shower of twigs and needles stung her cheek as a heavy limb, torn from the cypress, struck the ground beside her. She sprang forward in alarm, falling hands first into shallow water, hips higher than shoulders, palms sinking into muck. The slurry seeped through her fingers and she waited for the push of solid ground. It could not be far beneath. Soon the thickening ooze swallowed her wrists. And in horror she felt a cold, clamping pull on her forearms. The earth was gulping her down! Face inches from the water's surface, she screamed.

The wind delivered Claire's voice, in its terrifying timbre, to the men who on hearing it acted as one. No words were exchanged as Victor squatted to take up a paddle; as his father lunged into the canoe; as Robert pushed and shoved it far out into the water. In seconds father and son turned the canoe and headed toward Claire's island. Gliding swiftly alongside the thin strip of land, they saw the banked canoe but no sign of Claire. "Where are you?" bellowed Victor.

A frail voice, wilted with fear, responded. "Help."

Sitting at the bow, George leaned toward the sound. "That way!" he said, pointing beyond the island's length. Paddling vigorously, they rounded the island's far shore, speeding directly toward an exposed reef.

"We're going to hit!" cried George, back paddling in vain to avoid collision. Momentum thrust the canoe forward over rising silt and mud, absorbing its speed with a jolt. The canoe was grounded.

"Help me!"

George bolted from the bow toward the insistent plea straining to reach them. Victor raced over the hull, jumping struts like hurdles, exacting balance from the canoe. In an instant he trailed his father. Together they crossed the land bridge leading to the cypress and to Claire. Yet neither could at first make sense of what they saw. She appeared frozen in a crouching dive. Legs anchored to the ground above, arms and shoulders submerged, head twisted sideways against the water rising toward her nose.

On seeing her rescuers, Claire wailed like a lost fledgling.

No one noticed the Ivory-billed Woodpecker perched patiently above in the boughs of the cypress. He watched curiously as the two pulled the girl free and then, satisfied with this conclusion, flew away.

21

Return of the Black Bear

All were shaken by Claire's harrowing ordeal but perhaps more by what *might* have happened. This alternate ending, though avoided, especially distressed Claire. By moments only she had escaped death in a watery grave. She shuddered even now. During the drive back to camp, no one spoke to her of the Ivory-billed sighting.

Back at camp, despite the daylight, they started a campfire while she changed into dry clothes. "I'm not cold," she insisted of her shivering attacks. "Just nervous." Even so, in the heat of the day, she was made to sit before a blazing fire while the others busily occupied themselves. George and Victor packed the car while Robert, cell phone in hand, retreated inside the tent. Something about their behavior seemed suspicious to Claire, for though they tended lavishly to her needs, no one met her eyes. Eventually all three gathered before her, heads hanging like children forced to confess.

"What?" she cried, certain now of some new distress.

Both men looked to Victor, standing in the center and directly before Claire. Immediately crouching on bended knee, he reached for her hands. So distracting was this that she couldn't attend to his words.

"Claire, while you were gone, we saw the Ivory-bill."

Hearing the words "Ivory-bill," she quickly looked up from her hand, cradled in his. His dark brown eyes, tender with tears, gently held hers.

"What about the Ivory-bill?"

Victor dropped his head, exhaled heavily, and then looked again into her troubled expression.

"We saw him, while you were gone." Her face contracting in pain, he urgently added, "But we got him on video. You'll see it all."

Claire thrust violently upward, knocking Victor over, charging the men who parted to give her wide berth. No one tried to chase after, no one dared.

Robert Crawley sent his guests home on a commercial airline while he remained behind in Little Rock for press conferences on the rediscovery of the Ivory-billed Woodpecker. As a famed ornithologist and the group's leader, he was credited with the momentous find. That's not to say Victor wasn't acknowledged or that group photos weren't taken. Many were taken, both at camp and later in Little Rock.

Posing as part of this team greatly distressed Claire, conspicuous as the one member without an Ivory-bill tee shirt (hers a wet clump on the tent floor). She wore instead a black tee borrowed from Victor that mirrored her mood of betrayal. Beside her smiling colleagues, she looked a miserable, ghostly impostor, and anyone's attempts to make her feel less so only made her feel more the outcast. On the plane to Philadelphia, she huddled in the window seat, forehead pressed against its smudged pane. Later in the airport terminal, she drifted with a stiff neck distantly behind her companions.

George Arquetana would not again lose sight of his errant charge. At intervals he and Victor stopped to wait for Claire, strolling aimlessly through an anxious stream of travelers who either sputtered behind or speeded around her. Though sympathetic to her grief, the pair became increasingly preoccupied with their own anxieties, for Victor's mother Rose would now discover the truth of their trip to Arkansas. News of the woodpecker's rediscovery would be far reaching and fast traveling. How could they ever outrace it to Rose? More worrisome, how could they ever explain their deceit?

Baggage collected, the men pushed urgently toward the exit doors while Claire trailed after like a stray cat, desperate but fearful. George held open the door. "Come on, Claire. They'll be waiting for us in the car."

Waking from a self-absorbed stupor, she walked through the glass doors into hot, humid air, wondering, *Who will be waiting? Mother? Jerry?* A hopeful impulse tugged at her frown. She yanked and dragged the rolling luggage whose wheels could not now keep pace and nearly rammed Victor standing at the curbside pickup lane.

"Sorry," she muttered, a stubborn silence finally broken.

He looked to her with mild surprise.

"I can't wait to see Sammy," she said, swiftly glancing his way, confirming her intent to communicate. But Victor remained mute, as if expecting something more. She looked away, scanning the press of taxicabs, shuttles, and cars pulling into the pickup lane. Still he said nothing, eyes watching.

Swinging her arms in prelude to some announcement, she said, "Okay. I'm sorry for being such a brat."

Unmoved, Victor said, "Which time?"

Claire dropped her face to conceal its sour smile. Against rising tears she rocked her head, feeling silly and stupid. He was right to be cynical; throughout the trip she had been a horror. Victor instantly relented, grabbing her forearm. "I'm sorry, too, for being mean just now. We're square, okay?" Taking solace in his kindly eyes she sighed as George called, "They're here!"

Claire followed Mr. Arquetana's outstretched arm, seeking her mother's green coup. Then she saw and instantly despised *it*—the parrot-painted SUV. Where was her mother? Jerry? Dumbfounded, she watched as the garish vehicle pulled up before her and jettisoned Billy from its door. His face huge with joy, he sprang to the curb. "You goof!" he cried, whacking Victor on the back. "You found it!"

Knocked off balance, Victor choked, "Found what?"

"That woodpecker!"

Victor's face swelled with a grin that instantly popped. "Who told you?" he cried, picturing his mother in a rant. "Was

199

it in the paper?"

"I told him," said Glenn, smiling from across the vehicle's roof. His affable demeanor put Victor instantly at ease and Claire felt the steam of her resentment dissipate as with a cool wind. "Louise asked me to pick you up," he said, walking behind the car, "and of course she told us the incredible news." Claire cast shame-filled eyes downward, hoping to exclude herself from any congratulatory exchange.

Billy grabbed her baggage and with a casual chuckle said, "And I heard you were sucking swamp water, Belle."

Claire shot a panic-filled glance at him as all went quiet. Glenn stowed a piece of luggage in the vehicle before stepping toward the curb and Billy. "Really?" Glenn said quizzically, closing the distance between them. "Is that what you heard?" At six foot, six inches, he towered over the group, and Billy had to crane his neck to look up at him. The unfolding melodrama engrossed everyone, even Claire, who for a moment forgot about herself.

"No," Billy said, looking down. "You said she fell hands first into the water and got stuck in the sediment."

"That's right," Glenn said, resting a large hand on Billy's shoulder. "So how'd you get it so wrong just now?"

Billy shifted uncomfortably under its weight before delivering a coerced confession. "I was being a jerk," he said, looking off into the traffic. Then, squaring slumped shoulders and drawing a deep breath fouled by exhaust fumes, he turned to Claire. "Sorry, Belle."

Nodding mutely, she dove into the backseat, followed by Victor, who was mindful to act as buffer for the two antagonists. In this role, he felt most comfortable.

Despite the enormity of events at Stab Lake, the group thereafter spoke only briefly of the Ivory-bill sighting and not at all of Claire's incident. Of course, she knew the reason for this collective censure: no one wanted the 'outcast' to feel badly. Even Billy, she suspected, had spoken out of dumb habit more than nastiness. But knowing this did not make her feel any less dreadful. So as conversation turned to other topics, she stared sullenly out on the macadam and steel landscape through which they drove.

Too morose to care of what they spoke, Claire cowed before her worst fear—that the magic in her had died and she had killed it. The proof was evident: Victor, not she, had drawn the woodpecker. But how? Had he diluted her power by wearing the bird's image? If so, then the entire group had siphoned from it by wearing their shirts. She kicked the backseat in frustration.

"Hey!" cried Glenn, eyes raised within the rearview mirror in mock indignation. "You kicked me."

"Sorry!" She pulled the offending leg up to hug her knee. Claire slid a disgruntled glance to the watchful boys who quickly returned to talk of their Martian camp as she sank back into moody thoughts. More than a simple shirt had drawn the woodpecker to Victor. Like her, he had birds in his heart.

She knew so when hearing him whistle the melancholy notes of a meadowlark. Such exquisite fidelity to the bird's song could never be a function of vocal cords alone. His was a heart that resonated with the singer. The idea pained her because it meant she was less special. It meant that other people could draw birds to themselves, if only they knew.

Victor's father filled a lull in conversation with a casual question to Glenn. "Any updates on that break-in?"

The backseat occupants froze. Breathing suspended, each calculated what form of behavior would best appear natural. Claire released her knees into a leg stretch, Victor scooted forward to scratch his back, and Billy closed his gaping mouth. All averted their eyes, though inevitably these rolled toward Glenn like marbles on a downward slope. Intently they listened.

The billionaire's assistant spoke with detachment not equal to the subject. "Despite Robert's decision, I called in the police to investigate," he said, passing into the fast-moving traffic of the left lane. "And they identified the culprit as Clyde Hollow." Glenn met Billy's eyes in the rearview mirror and nodded. "Before anyone gets too awkward," his voice rose in volume with the announcement, "you should know that Billy and I have talked about this." The troubled teen lowered his gaze, an invitation for Victor and Claire to gawk, which they did, as Glenn continued. "And he understands that the best thing for his father is to be found."

Glenn's further conciliatory comments went mostly unattended by Billy's co-conspirators, busily calculating the situation: Hollow had been found out, but did Glenn and the police know that Billy was aiding his fugitive father? In the confines of the car, Claire and Victor could hardly ask and so tried to lift the answer from Billy's eyes, stubbornly cast downward. In the evolving conversation, however, they learned that the police were following various leads. No mention of Billy as an informant meant he hadn't told on his father.

"Can we stop for a moment?" Claire asked with a grimace, squeezing the calf of her leg. "I've got a cramp." Glenn obliged by pulling onto the shoulder of Highway 322 West, and Claire made a spectacle of limping away to stretch her muscles. The boys quickly followed. A swath of mowed grass bordering the paved shoulder sloped to a dry drainage ditch littered with debris. Within this channel the three gathered, barred entry into the woodlot beyond by a tangle of briar. "Where's your father?" Claire cried loudly over the whish of passing cars. "Has he gone yet?"

Instinctively all looked upward, shocked to see both men standing beyond the car, framed against the blue sky.

"Not so loud!" Billy hissed, swinging his head in disbelief. "Are you trying to get me in trouble?"

With no time to argue, they huddled, heads bowed, words spoken toward the ground. Billy outlined the situation. "He's leaving tomorrow, but I've got to get the money to him first."

"Tomorrow! But where?" demanded Claire.

"I'm not saying." Billy broke the huddle and jogged up to the waiting men. Victor turned away as well but Claire stalled to look into the trees tangled with wild grape vines. Over the harsh noise of cars ripping past, she strained to hear sounds of any bird hidden within the dark undergrowth. Nothing. Feeling empty as the canvas of her black tee, she stomped to the vehicle.

At 4:00 pm, without a backward glance, Billy bounded from the SUV toward his home with an urgency only Claire and Victor understood. At the door of the brick rancher stood his Aunt Lizzie, his father's sister, waving goodbye on behalf of her nephew. As he brusquely pushed past her, the stout woman twisted her wrist in final salute to those in the strange clown vehicle and then turned away, smiling fraily.

Soon they arrived to Victor's house, a simple white cottage with red shutters and a concrete stoop. As Glenn helped father and son pulled luggage from the cargo hold, Rose peered with aggrieved eyes through the bay window. Claire climbed into the front seat and propped an arm in its open window. A warm, floral-scented breeze caressed her face and she imagined a black bear waiting on the porch stoop as it had 12 years earlier for baby Victor. The large male bear rose on hind legs, lifting its long snout to the air. Seeming to catch her scent, he turned her way his huge shaggy head and rounded ears. His small eyes looked directly at her but then he was blocked from view by Victor, standing before her window.

The bear's image still printed on her mind, she squinted up at Victor. "I'll call you later," she said, referring to Billy's situation. He nodded with staring, unseeing eyes. Only then did she consider the confrontation awaiting him and his father inside. She had heard their covert exchanges on the plane but at the time cared little. Now she wanted to extend Victor some comfort. "It's going to be all right," she said earnestly, nodding toward the front door. "Your bear guide is waiting on the stoop."

Victor twisted about, charged and alert. The stoop was empty but for his mother's rigid form, filling the doorway. He turned back to Claire, eyes eager and full.

A Strange Dream

Glenn parked outside the country store to the sound of Sammy's siren howls amplified at once by Moon Doggy. Through the bay window, the shaggy-headed sheepdog watched Claire race toward the porch steps.

"Sammy!" she cried, slipping over the banister separating the cement porch from its wood plank counterpart. She dropped opposite his black nose behind the breath-fogged windowpane and crooned, "I'm home!" Ears perked and head cocked, Sammy stared through the fringe of his mop-like bangs and then wailed to the ceiling.

Claire flung open the front door, squatting to absorb her dog's furious affection. Even so he knocked her to the living room floor, cold nose prodding her neck, sticky tongue grazing her skin. She squealed with delight as he snorted his devout, zealous love. On the store side of the swinging door, Moon Doggy yowled against his exclusion until a loud swish spit him into the room.

After a two-canine greeting Claire surfaced much the happier, stumbling into the store and eager for a family reception of hearty hugs. She was however surprised to find these same affections shared with Glenn. It didn't make sense. Why would her mother and Jerry embrace a near stranger? The answer, though not immediate, revealed itself in her mother's repeated, discreet glances toward the especially tall man. Her mother seemed fascinated with the oddity of looking up. And Jerry tugged at Glenn's forearm like a willful child. "Sit down, sit down," he said, coaxing the man toward the storeroom break table. "I get a crick in the neck just looking up at you." Claire watched these displays with wonderment and a good dose of jealousy, especially when Sammy offered Glenn his best hind swaggering welcome.

Ragged emotions torn anew, Claire demanded, "Come on, Sammy!" She shoved the swinging door inward to the residence, saying, "We're going to our room." Delighted for the invitation, sheepdog and beagle bounded with nail-tapping alacrity over the linoleum while Louise called after for her to get some much needed rest. "And later this evening you can tell us all about the trip."

Claire stomped angrily up the enclosed, curving stairwell. She resented their seeming disinterest despite relief in delaying an account of her many humiliations. "Yeah, like I can rest," she fumed, collapsing onto her bed, crowded instantly with two smelly, over-excited dogs. Such joy as theirs was not conducive to her brooding mood, so she pushed them off, again and again, until they relented, sighing together into a heap onto the rug.

In the quiet of her room, the weight of Clyde Hollow's escape plans began to bear down on her. Billy's plan to meet with his desperate father, nearly always drunk, was a terrible idea. Yet how could she stop him without disclosing the entire truth? Clyde Hollow was a super creep, but she felt unprepared to be the cause of his imprisonment. Fitfully she rolled atop the covers, from one shoulder to the other, until sounds of canine snoring gradually soothed her to sleep and then into a dream.

In that gauzy realm, she knelt on a bank above a pool of milky brown water. Over the creamy calm, she lowered her face, hoping to glimpse beneath its surface. She saw instead a faithful reflection, clearly as if in a mirror, but the eyes staring into her own were golden.

"How odd," she said. "I'm wearing my colored lenses but my reflection isn't." She could not long ponder this mystery because beside her reflected visage appeared another—that of an Ivory-billed Woodpecker. It loomed larger than life, as big as her face, with sunflower eyes beneath a blazing red pompadour. The cartoon quality startled and engaged her. Viewed face on, not in profile, the bird's long ivory-colored bill appeared foreshortened, like a stout snout, which surprisingly began to speak.

"We've had a message for you for some time," said the bird, its voice female, one Claire recognized but couldn't identify. "So why haven't you been listening?"

Claire felt unjustly criticized. "I am too listening," she said, pushing her face closer to the water. "Tell me now." The reflection however shrank from her into a tiny speck but before disappearing said, snidely, "You're too busy sucking swamp water." As though commanded, the cloudy surface rose quickly to smother her face and Claire woke with a gasp. A deep breath stifled the panic and her face sunk again into the foam pillow, body still drugged with fatigue. While she slept, taunted or chased in dreamscapes, Victor confronted the waking world in the person of his mother.

With harsh eyes Rose had met him and his father at the door, withholding complaint until their odd transport pulled away. Its presence spoke of some undeclared event, one outside her granted permission. "Explain that ridiculous vehicle, please," she had said, voice stern, gaze averted. Her face, its dark brows knit beneath a stalk-dry crop of bleached hair, looked waxen and drawn.

George dropped his baggage to the floor, shoulders slumping. "It's a long story, Rose," he said in an affable but weary tone. "I'll make coffee and we'll tell you all about it." Rose could not wait, harassing her husband with questions at the kitchen counter as he tended the coffee maker. Seated at the table, in the corner of the small square room, Victor watched, his mind clinging to Claire's parting words: *Your bear guide is waiting on the stoop.* This simple statement had affected him profoundly. Instantly, dread had leapt from his shoulders like some heavy rodent. Even now, he felt confident of a positive outcome.

Rose vented much of her agitation during the coffee making, prolonged by her husband for this very purpose.

Over the years, he had developed tactics for diffusing her frenzied states. By the time he set two mugs onto the table, she had settled onto a seat, spine straight, fingers entwined into a nervous knot. A summer breeze billowed the kitchen curtains, their cotton fibers cast radiant by the late day sun. George inhaled deeply of the breeze, gathering energy and inspiration. He stood behind a spindle-backed chair, cupping his hands to its thick, egg-shaped finials. His serious dark eyes landed softly onto his wife's.

"Your son is the first person in over half a century to both see and record—in an incontrovertible video—the Ivory-billed Woodpecker."

Rose recognized the declaration as momentous, though she knew nothing of the bird. The confusion irritated her. Looking to Victor, anchoring her palms flat to the table, she said, "What is he talking about?" But Victor likewise sat surprised. Only on hearing his father's pronouncement did he appreciate his part. He sat silently, stunned and smiling.

George reclaimed her attention. "To explain, we have to give you background," he said, sitting now, pulling his seat closer to hers. She shook her head against this, not willing to postpone the interrogation. But George pressed pass her objections, his voice modulating in the enticing tones of an expert storyteller. He spoke of the Ivory-bill, long believed extinct, and of Robert Crawley's efforts to find it. Rose restrained herself to listen, curious to know more about the visiting billionaire, lately in the local newspaper. She could not yet anticipate the celebrity's link to her family. When this connection became apparent, when George confessed his decision to conceal a trip to Arkansas, Rose erupted from her chair shouting, "You did what?"

Pacing the small floor area, she remonstrated shrilly against them, hands flung to the air. Yet to father and son, her tirade seemed somehow theatrical, poorly acted rather than felt. Missing was the unseeing stare, cast about as if suddenly blind. A mannerism of her most incensed states, its absence meant she was reachable.

Offering profuse apologies, the two admitted to their sins—most heinous being, as she described, "a callous disregard and disrespect for me!" Nor did they attempt to defend themselves, for to do so would only incite her more. They instead accepted her denouncements, waiting for the emotional storm to pass. When finally it did, George coaxed out her curiosity. "I can see, Rose," he said, standing, "that you're too upset to hear the rest of the story."

Blustery and righteous, she pushed downward on his shoulder. "Sit!" she commanded. "I want to hear it all, now."

George took care to recreate the suspense and sensory detail of their swampland adventure. Nor did he exclude elements of danger, as when they floated past the mating Cottonmouths. Most especially he emphasized their son's contributions—how one moment Victor coolly filmed the Ivory-billed Woodpecker (despite Robert's hysteria) and the

211

next helped to execute a flawless rescue of Claire.

During this narrative, Rose lost her indignation within a rampant growth of pride. It sprouted from her heart and blossomed in her eyes, so long withered from fear and mistrust. "Victor," she said, eyes now luxuriant with tears. "I'm so proud of you."

When later that evening Victor received an anxious call from Claire, he had ample good news to share. "My mother's like a different person!" he said in a giddy voice. "And you won't believe this—Dad's still here! They're in the living room right now talking and laughing." He spoke in a half whisper from behind his bedroom door, opened a crack to confirm this report.

Though happy for Victor, Claire couldn't long listen to the details of his mother's wonderful but strange behaviors. She wanted instead to discuss Billy, insistent they do something to stop him from meeting with his fugitive father. Here, yet again, Victor provided incredible news. "I've taken care of it," he said, plopping to the bed on his back. He waited for her astonished reaction.

"How?" she demanded, not at all convinced. Like Victor she spoke from her bed, only moments earlier having woken from a long nap. Already it was dark outside her window and the dogs were restless at her bedside, demanding to be let out of the room.

Victor kept her in suspense, digressing to discuss the reason for his recent good fortune. "You were right, Tahwach, about the black bear. He was waiting here to help me. But however did you see him?"

"I didn't see him, Victor. I imagined it," she nearly shouted, annoyed at his delay in answering her question. Crawling from her bed, she opened the door to let out the dogs.

Victor knew otherwise, informed by his father's explanation of Claire's gifts and her animal spirit—the Red-tailed Hawk—that gave her extraordinary sight, even into the spiritual realm. "No, you did see my bear spirit. You just don't know it."

Claire inhaled to speak but stalled. An image of the Ivory-billed Woodpecker filled her mind. Had she seen it, as well, in spirit? Heavily she exhaled. "Would you please just tell me what you did about Billy?"

Victor quickly obliged, explaining that he had called Billy and convinced him not to meet with his father at the agreed upon time and location. Instead he suggested that Billy go early with a note and the money, placing these in plain sight, using as a marker some bright colored piece of clothing. "That way," he explained, "Billy can give his father the money without putting himself in danger."

"Victor," Claire gushed with much relief, "that's a brilliant idea."

213

"I know," he said happily.

"And you're sure he'll do it?" She wanted to be completely convinced.

"Pretty sure," Victor said. "We talked for a while about it. Billy's afraid of his father but knows he must help. This way he can without worrying what his crazy father might do."

Claire sighed. "I feel so much better now." For a second she basked in the unexpected comfort of his news. Then alert and energized, she ended their conversation. "I've got to go, Victor. Mom and Jerry want me downstairs."

Urgently, before she could disconnect, he added. "I'll call you tomorrow," knowing that only after he and Billy had executed the *real* plan would he reveal it to Claire.

23

Stopping to Listen

The plan as described to Claire wasn't an outright lie, rather one of omission. Victor withheld certain cogent elements, including his part in the scheme. He would accompany Billy to the drop off location where, after planting the money, they would conceal themselves to observe the "pick up." Billy would not agree to Victor's plan without witnessing his father find the money. And because Victor didn't trust Billy, he insisted on going along. But on one point both boys agreed: Claire should play no role.

That night Victor went to bed content, imagining his bear spirit beside him and knowing that in the morning he would guide the way. Claire, too, went to bed with an eased mind, no longer dreading the coming day. Neither was she as galled by recent events, having treated her wounded ego to the balm of maternal love. With quiet attention Louise had listened to her daughter's frantic narrative as they lay on chaise lounges above the cold, dew-drenched grass. Like a testifying defendant, Claire was at times tremulous, often embarrassed, and sometimes resentful. But as the night swelled with stars, she lost interest in the story. And the stellar fires ablaze in her pupils consumed all agitation until she again felt like herself.

The next morning Louise's customers were hungry for more than pie and coffee. Everyone wanted to know whether

Claire had seen her Ivory-billed Woodpecker. Mercifully, Louise protected her daughter from these inquiries, assigning her to kitchen duties and enlisting Jerry's help to wait tables. In this role, the elder appeared supremely suited, efficient and friendly. In fact, he was so conspicuously happy that Helen Whiner demanded to know the reason. She grabbed the back ties of his apron as he hurried past her table, and in a petulant manner said, "What are you smirking about?"

Jerry turned swiftly, a full pot of coffee orbiting at bended arm's length. Dipping the pot over Helen's empty cup, he nodded to the sunny day outside. "What's not to smile about, Helen?" The instant she twisted toward the window, he plucked from her scalp a loose bobby pin, releasing its springy coil. "You should try it sometime," he added, winking merrily before turning abruptly away. He left her staring after him in astonishment, a hand clamped over the escaped curl.

Jerry's feisty humor was part of a larger, brighter disposition born of recent events. The police investigation of the chateau break-in had established Clyde Hollow as the culprit, thereby clearing the elder caretaker of any suspicion. Jerry carried his friend's exoneration like a personal triumph. Moreover Ben's recovery, though slow, showed daily improvements. Closer to home, Jerry watched with unreserved pleasure as Glenn made tentative overtures toward Louise. He heartily approved of this sensible, young man of principle, so unlike his employer.

After the morning rush, Claire hurriedly crossed the storeroom, pulling off a work apron. Pushing open the swinging door, she called upstairs for the dogs. The summons triggered a short bout of howling, followed by the heavy thud of two dogs dropping from her bed to the floor. "I'm taking the dogs for a walk."

Louise stood closing a folding table to store until the next day. The morning sun no longer shone in the front windows. "I don't want you in those woods again until that lunatic Hollow is caught."

"What?" Claire dropped her arm bracing the swinging door to march toward her mother. "That could take months!" she bawled, knowing it might never happen if Hollow successfully escaped. Nonplussed, Louise handed the folded table to Jerry, to whom Claire now entreated as he carried it toward the summer kitchen. "Tell her, Jerry! Hollow's long gone by now."

The old man knew better than to take sides and suggested a compromise: that he escort Claire on such outings until Hollow was caught. Louise conceded and Claire won her demand to that day visit the outcrop with him to see the hawks.

Clyde Hollow stumbled through the woodland undergrowth en route to his rendezvous with Billy. Splatters of noontime sun filtering through the trees blazed against his light-sensitive eyes, squeezed into slits. Time and again he fell into holes hidden beneath a lush weave of ground vines, mumbling curses as he crawled back to his feet. Since the billionaire's return to the chateau, Clyde had been homeless. And sleeping inside a dank, dark cave was no picnic, even with the sleeping bag stolen from Jerry's cabin. Moreover he lived in constant fear of discovery, straying never far from his pipeline, Billy. The only thing that made any of this bearable was bourbon, and now he was out.

Plodding forward with a heavy hangover, Clyde tried not to think about his toes, pinched into hiking boots half a size too small. While Crawley's clothes, stolen from his chateau, fit well enough, the boots didn't. Yet his own shoes had disintegrated, and his son's were far too large, so he had none other to wear, not until he could steal a pair. Once he was on the road and heading west, stealing shoes would be his number one priority. No. Bourbon. Then shoes.

Billy and Victor arrived at the drop off location, the outhouse behind Jerry's cabin, at 11:00 am, well before the designated time, which was noon.

"We're nuts to be back here again." Victor spoke to Billy, standing inside the outhouse, through a large knothole in its sidewall. The rustic bathroom facility was just big enough to walk into, turn around, and sit onto a warped gray board with a large oval hole. But Billy wasn't sitting; he was stuffing a backpack filled with provisions for his father onto a wide shelf above his head that formed the structure's ceiling. Long ago this space under the roof had become a nesting place for Eastern Phoebes. Old feathers and dried poop showered down onto Billy's face. "Yuchhh!" He spit the debris from his mouth. "This is worse then cleaning the pigeon loft."

Victor pounded on the wall for emphasis. "Hurry up!" He glanced into the surrounding woods. "We've got to find a place to hide before he gets here."

"Done!" Billy stepped out of the outhouse brushing the dirt from his clean brown hair, recently cut and styled on Glenn's suggestion. An oily pad no longer hung over his right eye. From a clean side part, a graceful sweep of bangs dipped to below his eyebrow but did not cover his glass eye. Victor could not yet help staring at this marvel, finally revealed to the world.

Since they didn't know from what direction Billy's father would approach, they had to be concealed from all angles. Hurriedly racing a perimeter, they found nothing. "We've got to get out of here," Victor said, poking his head inside the cabin's weathered walls, gray and brittle. "There's no place to hide."

"Oh yes there is," Billy crowed, shoving past him into the cabin. His idea was to hide inside to keep watch from its windows.

"But what if your father comes inside?"

"Simple. We hop out a window."

Hours after the sun had reached its zenith and the small gravel parking lot lay in shadow, Jerry and Claire crossed the road to the long narrow pasture bordering the woods. They followed the winding, mowed path while the dogs plunged into the high pasture grasses. Sammy's plumed tail marked their progress like a periscope above the sea while clouds of gnats pulsed in the warm afternoon air.

They stopped at the mighty white oak for a brief check of their provisions and general readiness. When hiking to the outcrop, Jerry called this sprawling giant "base camp" to magnify their sense of adventure. Below them the creek ran full, freshening the air with sounds of water cascading over a short falls. "So what's our bird for today?" he said, feigning surprise to see the empty canvas of her sunny yellow tee shirt, though having noted it earlier.

Claire had forgotten the shirt hidden beneath a bib apron all morning and was unprepared for the inquiry. "I turn 12 next week, Jerry," she said, turning her face toward the furrowed, ash-gray bark. Picking a loose piece, cold rebuke in her tone, she added, "I don't have to wear bird shirts every day like some little kid."

As Jerry patted his chest pocket for a pipe, Claire stumbled over the oak's raised roots to the other side of the trunk to sit, stubborn and silent. She heard the striking match and then smelled the smoke of his favorite cherry-flavored tobacco. "Seems to me—" he paused to take a deep draw and then to exhale—"that what you say is partially true." He circled the tree to look down on her. "But I suspect the whole truth has something to do with you and that woodpecker."

Mention of the woodpecker brought sudden tears to her eyes. Everything unsaid to her mother the night before rose within as a boiling spring. "The birds don't want me, Jerry," she cried, burying her face into boney knees. Lifting it again, she wailed, "And you were wrong!"

This dramatic accusation had an unintended effect. It made Jerry smile. Turning aside his face to conceal its amusement, he took a deep draw on his pipe. "How so?" he said, keeping the query short to avoid a chuckle.

Absorbed in the tragedy, Claire continued her complaint. "You said it wasn't the shirt; you said it was my heart that brought the birds," she sucked air in with sobs. "Yet everyone saw the Ivory-bill," she shouted, "everyone but me!" Case made, she dropped her head, shoulders hopping to her muffled cries.

"Hmmm …" Jerry loudly mulled over the evidence. "I see." Pipe clenched in his teeth, he said, "And you kept the woodpecker in your heart?"

Claire raised her head, considering the question. For seconds she said nothing until lifting a woeful face. "I suppose."

"You don't know?"

Bracing her hand against the oak's rough bark, she pushed upward. "I know," she said defensively, dusting dirt from her seat bottom. "I did keep it in my heart, but not—not deeply, not like Big Red."

Following her from the oak, Jerry said, "Nothing wrong there," as they reached the path parallel to the creek below. After a short distance they headed down a rocky, sloping grade to the creek, where Sammy and Moon Doggy waded into their favorite water hole.

"The thing is," she said with a sigh, sinking suddenly onto her haunches. "I was just trying to impress Robert." She picked up a stone to throw into the creek.

"And?"

"And," she dropped her head, "I told him about my power." To this, Jerry said nothing. Provoked by his silence, she bounced to her feet, nimbly darting over the stepping-stones in the creek. The dogs, their coats surging water, charged the steep hillside opposite through stately hemlock trees. Reaching the top, ears perked, the pair peered down for their companions and then, with rolling energy, leaped away.

"I think I've pieced this together, little girl," Jerry said, stowing the pipe into his pocket for the creek crossing. Claire watched as he trod cautiously over the narrow span of wet rocks. "You're saying the woodpecker snubbed you for spilling the secret to that fool Crawley."

Expressed so succinctly, the idea sounded stupid even to Claire. "More than just that," she pouted. "I was so set on showing off, I didn't respect my bond with the birds. That … and I haven't been listening."

Jerry hopped up out of the creek bed. "Well, let's stop to listen right now."

Claire was about to say, "That's not what I meant" but didn't because she didn't *know* what she meant, the statement flew from her of its own accord, and because what Jerry implied was true. She hadn't been listening to the birds, not like she used to. So for the first time that day, she listened. Though a drowsy part of the warm afternoon, many songbirds were singing, their cheery whistles and ecstatic trills as refreshing as cold creek water flowing over bare feet.

"Sounds like the birds can't stay mad at you," Jerry said, with a wink. Turning to face the steep wooded grade, he stroked his beard. "And I'm not convinced that woodpecker ever was mad at you. Weren't you the first to hear it knock?"

Claire bounded up the hill ahead of her elder like a Billy goat to look down upon him. She crouched in a shallow depression padded with Hemlock needles. "Yes," she said, eyes brightly expectant. "I heard the Ivory-bill knock twice— but no one else did."

"And since when has anyone had better hearing than you?"

To this truth she nodded emphatically. "So?"

"So looks like you can add one Ivory-billed Woodpecker to your Life List!"

This declaration so surprised Claire that she fell off the perch of her haunches. On his angled ascent, Jerry reached out a thick, coarse hand to pull her up, likewise steadying himself. "Now tell me you didn't already think of that."

An hour past the scheduled rendezvous, under the gaze of watchful eyes from inside the cabin, Clyde Hollow limped onto Jerry's property. Wracked with a splitting skull and tortured toes, he gave little thought to Billy, concerned only with finding the money. After plundering the backpack to find it, he sunk to the ground in relief.

Despite what Billy had told Victor, he needed to witness the "pick-up" for more reasons than assuring that his father found the money: to see his father, possibly for the last time, and hopefully to observe some sign of regret at his absence. To promote this expression, Billy had written a long, heart-felt letter, but his father tossed it from the backpack like so much package stuffing, intent only on finding the money. Billy turned his face from Victor, embarrassed by the swell of burning tears, his glass eye bathed without sensation. "Let's get out of here," he said, jumping from the back window. Victor was quick to follow.

Clyde found and thirstily drank from one of several water bottles stuffed inside the backpack along with a dozen hardboiled eggs, apples, cheese, and a bag of large, hard pretzels, perfect foods for the road. He smiled. In the upper compartment he found toothpaste and a brush, shaving lotion and a razor, a soap bar and deodorant—exactly what he needed. And he hooted with glee on discovering three packs of cigarettes and a lighter. Tearing open a pack with shaking hands, he hurriedly lit one, slumping to the ground for a smoke and a moment of contentment.

An hour later when he woke, Clyde decided to nurse his hangover for the rest of the day and take to the road the next. Well provisioned now, he felt less urgency to leave and began a slow, tortuous hike in Crawley's boots back to his dank cave at the base of a rock outcrop. A mere hole in the cliff side, it was high enough to sit in and deep enough to sleep in and thus adequate for his current needs. A country boy, Clyde knew how to tell time by the sun. Trudging through a thicket of mountain laurel, he squinted against its merciless blaze, still high in the sky. Then he heard it. A rattle. His heart jumped; he froze mid stride, left heel lifted. Looking down he could see only pulsating spots imprinted on his retina by the sun. If not sober, he would have lumbered onward, blind or not, snake be damned. But he was sober, and he was afraid, terribly afraid.

An outsider happening onto this scene would have perceived the odd spectacle of a somewhat deranged-looking, thoroughly unkempt man, in fashionable sports attire, striking a wobbling pose in a field of mountain laurel. And this is exactly what Jerry saw—at first.

Chapter 23

"That's Billy's dad," called Claire from behind. They had entered the laurel field opposite of Hollow's route and stood facing him from a straight-line distance of 75 feet.

"Stay behind me, Claire," Jerry ordered, quickly surveying the situation. Hollow carried no rifle, lessening the immediate threat, but desperate men were prone to desperate acts. "Hollow," Jerry barked. "What in the world are you doing?"

"Snake," he whimpered, his balance ever more tottering. "Rattler," he cried pleadingly.

Issuing to Claire a stern command to stay rooted, Jerry plunged through the hedges as Clyde risked another downward glance. Vision cleared, he could finally see his adversary—a buff-colored timber rattler, triangular head raised and swaying, vertical pupils vacantly staring, poised to strike. Startled, he lost balance and pitched forward, right arm and hand diving toward the snake that instantly struck, sinking poisonous fangs into his bicep.

Hollow howled in anguish, not pain, for it was certainly a death sentence. The side of his face hit the ground and he watched the rattler whipping away. Jerry was bending over him. "Did you get hit?" the old man cried.

"In the arm."

Straightening up, grabbing his thick, coarse hair, Jerry shook his head. "Good Lord! Good Lord! What are we going to do?" Neither he nor Claire carried a cell phone and every minute counted. Panic gripped him.

"Hey!" A masculine voice called from the stand of white pine bordering the outcrop. "What's going on?"

"Is that my Billy boy?" Clyde cried, raising his cheek stamped with twigs and stones to holler, "BILL-E-E-E-E-E."

This unexpected aid jolted Jerry into action. He unbuckled his belt to use as a tourniquet, slipping it around and above the snakebite on Hollow's thin, pale arm. Focused entirely on the task, he said nothing but "snakebite" to the three faces soon hovering over the scene. With the task done, he stood to give orders. "Billy you stay here with your father and me while Victor and Claire run for help."

"No!" cried Hollow, twisting up from the ground, looking frantically for his son. "Billy, you go!" He grabbed his son's hand, pulling him down, closer to his bloodshot eyes glazed with pain and fear. "I trust only you to save my life."

Billy felt his scalp contract in a tightening of resolve. "I'll save you, dad," he said, bursting upward, clambering over Victor squatting beside him. "Out of my way!" he shrieked lunging forward, stumbling through the laurel.

"Wait for us!" cried Victor in pursuit, with Claire delaying long enough to get instructions before leaping after like a doe through the thicket.

24

Soaring

Claire hid behind the row of tall, pointed cedar trees lining the curving stone bench to re-read her Mamo's letter. No one would miss her for a few moments. Sounds of laughter spilled from the upper terrace of the chateau, where dozens of guests were enjoying a late afternoon garden party to celebrate Robert and his team's rediscovery of the Ivory-billed Woodpecker. From a deep front pocket in her flowing, floral skirt, she pulled the single sheet, reverently opening its many folds.

Dearest Child,

Despite what you may be hearing, your Mamo is of sound mind, well, no less sound than ordinary. Ha! I've been fretting your grandmother of late with my insistence that you visit us <u>soon</u>. It's not right that I haven't seen you for nearly 4 years! And, Claire, there's something else, something important you need to know about who you are, why you're different, and what it all means. Your grandmother made me swear not to tell you until you were 12, mature enough to handle the responsibility. I'll explain everything when I see you, but please, please, *Hurry!*

I love you— *Mamo*

Claire stared at the print of her great-grandmother's ancient typewriter willing more meaning from its too few words.

. . . who you are, why you're different, and what it all means.

"I'm Claire Belle," she said softly, "and I'm different because I have a pigment disorder." Biting her lower lip, she thought hard to answer the last bit, the only true riddle. "It means that people look at me differently. That I look at myself differently." Though true, this wasn't her Mamo's meaning. Of that she was certain. To coax more from the message, she read it aloud, jolted at the final word, *Hurry!* At once she knew: the Ivory-bill's voice in her dream was Mamo's! As was the voice in her bizarre blackout at the outcrop.

"There you are!" exclaimed Victor, bounding into her private sanctuary, an embodiment of joy. He plopped onto the bench beside her. "What are you reading?" he said, peering over her shoulder but giving her no pause to answer before calling into the cloudless sky. "Can you believe that my mother is here with my father?" He slapped his thighs and hopped back onto his feet. "It's unbelievable!"

Possessed of her own revelation, eyes fixed and staring, Claire appeared properly amazed. "It's wonderful," she said, slipping the letter back into her pocket. She smiled up at him, straddling a gulf between inner and outer realities—her mind locked on the puzzling epiphany and Victor, in navy dress pants and a white short-sleeved shirt, on the lush lawn before her. Grabbing her hands, he yanked her upward into his

229

elation and arms, hugging her hard. "I'm so happy," he said, voice sweet as a child's.

Claire felt his emotion through her burning eyes and short breath. "It's like a miracle," she whispered, feeling comfort in his embrace. Pulling apart, they exchanged shy smiles with misty eyes. Victor turned again to the bench to sit.

"It was the trip that did it," he said, grinning with wonder as Claire sat beside him. "Mom now sees me as some kind of hero who can take care of himself. And—" He jumped again from the bench. "She's even got dad to put out a suet feeder for the woodpeckers. Can you believe that?"

"I can't believe it," Claire said, matching with volume his emotional intensity. "Is your father moving home then?"

"No, they're taking things slowly," he said more somberly, settling down again beside her, dark eyes shifting in thought. "But that's good, right?" Claire nodded heartily, noting in those same eyes a sudden playful cast foretelling a change of topic. "It's your turn," he said, words tinted with a tease. "What about your mom and Glenn?"

On this topic there wasn't much to tell. "I noticed something between them as soon as we got back from Arkansas but was distracted by Billy's situation." Victor understood. Everyone in Tipple now knew the sensational story of Clyde Hollow—drunkard, deadbeat dad, and recent fugitive—who nearly got away but for one timber rattler. The pit viper had injected a large dose of venom into Hollow's upper arm, which momentarily began to swell and bruise. Yet help was fast coming because, good to his promise, Billy ran more swiftly than ever before. And soon a life-flight helicopter landed at the base of the outcrop. After a few days in the hospital, Hollow was transported to another institution, the county prison.

"But what about your mom's date with Glenn today?" persisted Victor, who wanted more substantial facts.

Claire had no opportunity to explain, that instant summoned by Glenn from the terrace wall. "Get up here you two," he called, his strong voice easily reaching the hidden pair exchanging grins. "Robert has an important announcement." Victor bounced up, chuckling. "That man dearly loves his announcements."

To the brisk tempo of Bach's Brandenburg Concerto No. 2 in F major, the pair entered a stream of guests retracing their steps to the upper terrace. Included in this group were the mayor and her husband and their district's state representative and his spouse. Claire and Victor, however, saw only colorfully attired women in sundresses and hats escorted by impeccably dressed men. All wore too much cologne. Heading up the stairwell to the first terrace, they were zoomed by several Ruby-throated Hummingbirds. The women gaily shrieked as these tiny birds, glittering green and red in the sun, traced sweeping arcs in the air above their heads. "Must be your perfume," joked the mayor's husband, a middle-aged man as stout and plump as his wife. "Or their bright dresses," contributed the state representative. A dignified elder, he raised a forearm against the buzzing dynamos. Only Claire and Victor knew the real reason: the pretty pair of hummingbirds stenciled on her delicate white tee shirt.

When the assembly of 40 guests was at last seated at tables crowding the upper terrace, the host stood by the kitchen entrance upon a wooden crate. Clinking a silver spoon against a crystal water goblet, he quickly gained their attention. "I hope you're having a good time and have enjoyed our delicious meal catered by Tipple's very own Grace Huntley." The kitchen door briskly opened and a young woman with a toothy smile and white bib apron nodded to the applauding crowd before ducking back inside. Robert continued. "And here's hoping the earlier tour I gave of my chateau didn't disappoint." Again the guest applauded on cue. "But now for the real purpose of our celebration: to share highlights of my team's rediscovery of the Ivory-billed Woodpecker." A rousing round of applause smothered Victor's audible sigh of resignation. Yet again he must suffer through one of Crawley's long-winded lectures.

Seated at another table by the terrace wall with her mother and Glenn, Claire shared Victor's boredom. She tried to listen but Robert's words quickly became a loud droning in her ears. She studied instead his lovely self attired in white seersucker trousers and a cobalt cotton shirt, yet still he failed to hold her interest. Somewhere, somehow, she had lost her infatuation. From the lower terrace, the marble sculpture of Ku-Khain called up to her. Claire gazed down upon the monument of her beloved hawk, wishing she were at the outcrop. According to Victor, the Red-tailed Hawk was her animal spirit guide. So what did that make Ku-Khain? Her *living* animal guide? If so, to where would the raptor guide her?

Claire wandered within a daydream pondering this question when woke by a tapping on her arm. "Pay attention," her mother instructed, leaning inward to speak confidentially. "This part has to do with you." Claire obediently sat upright, eyes focused on her host, who at that instant extended a hand in her direction and with it the eyes of the entire assembly. Everyone was clapping in response to his comment, which she missed entirely but pretended otherwise, nodding and smiling graciously until Robert again drew their attention.

What next he said truly startled her. A leading birding institute was honoring the rediscovery team (and their close family members) with an all expenses paid trip to a premier birding location. "And you get to choose from three places," said Robert clasping and pumping his hands, a mannerism Claire thought he entirely overused. "Costa Rica, the Florida Everglades, or Ireland!" With mention of Ireland, Claire audibly squealed, causing everyone to look her way with a smile or chuckle. "So team members—Victor, George, and Claire," he said, motioning for them to stand in the tradition of any game show. "What will it be?"

Chapter 24

Victor looked first to his parents, obtaining an unspoken permission for what he then said, looking across the crowded tables to Claire. "Dad and I think Claire should choose."

Knees sinking in relief, eyes melting in appreciation, she choked out one word: "Ireland!"

After a hearty hug from her mother and a shoulder pat from Glenn, Claire pushed through the tables, tripping over legs and knocking into tables, the clatter of dishes sounding behind her. She could not get to Victor quickly enough, finally stumbling into his arms. "Now I can't believe it!" she said, hugging him gratefully, her pale cheek pressed against his brown one. "We're going to Ireland."

The final event of the celebration was a showing of the Ivory-billed Woodpecker video, which Claire had seen twice since her return two weeks prior. Victor had seen the video as often but being its author was expected to be present. So was she, for that matter, but while filing into the library with the other guests, Claire felt an impulse to lag behind. And this impulse developed instantly into a full-blown plan: to revisit the chateau's south tower where, on Robert's earlier guided tour, she first saw the perch used by her Ku-Khain, then trained as a young hawk in falconry.

Drifting to the side, Claire slowly stepped backward from the arched doorway. As the last person filed past, she glanced over her shoulder. No one in view. Quickly she crept across the marble floor to French doors leading to the interior courtyard. While on Robert's tour, she had marveled at this precious piece of outdoors growing within the chateau. A perfect square, the courtyard consisted of a central mound herb garden scenting the air with a mix of oils, lavender being most prominent. Following the stone path around the garden, she passed a wall of ivies and ferns, the sound of falling water within their tangles, until reaching the doors opposite her entry.

Pushing through these, she found herself outside the sitting room, with its spectacle of white pedestals and life-sized bird statues. Victor and she had first seen the room as trespassers, peering from the outside in. On the tour, they saw it again: the Winter Birds Room. Robert Crawley, world famous ornithologist, displayed in painted statuary the birds of Pennsylvania in a total of six rooms, each organized on a theme. Thus the library hosted the Birds of Prey, while Robert reserved for his bedroom the Birds of the Forest. Though loudly praising these extraordinary exhibits, his guests quietly murmured of their host's exceeding extravagance. But, then, how else did billionaires spend their money?

The courtyard shared its light and greenery with an inside hallway that opened into a domed-ceiling foyer. Here, finally, on the south corner was access to the spiral stone stairway. She flew toward it, fearful that one of the caterers might spot her. Inside the stairwell and out of sight, she finally relaxed. Climbing the expansive cylindrical well of limestone, she looked out through each casement window to the changing views beyond. Pausing to look through these, she thought again of her recent revelation—that it was Mamo's voice, in dreams and daydreams, urging her to hurry. Even more odd was that she should imagine the birds to carry this message. Whatever could it mean? With little time to ponder, she pushed onward, knowing that their trip to Ireland would reveal all.

At the second floor, she stalled at the arched, ornate door leading to Robert's room. With the other guests, she had marveled at the many statues of warblers, all perfectly painted, perched about his room, not on pedestals but within a network of sculptured branches and greenery, stunning to see. Should she see them again? Hand poised over the doorknob, she paused. No. There wasn't time. Upward to the roof she hurried.

At the top of the stairwell, another imposing arched door opened onto a circular parapet, renovated to serve as an aviary for Robert's Alexandra. Roofed and screened, the tower top served as the young hawk's home while not in training. A portion of a petrified oak, its trunk and several lateral limbs, served as her perch. Claire stared at this feature, imagining a young Ku-Khain tamed to subservience. But not for long. By Robert's own admission, she had stayed with him less than a year, one day flying from the perch of his arm, not to return.

Outside the screened enclosure, a narrow walkway circled the tower, extending beyond the pointed roof. Through a screen door, Claire passed into this open place to view the surrounding landscape. In the West the sun dipped toward the horizon, only moments left as a full, glorious orb of fire.

Strolling about the tower, staring off into the sky, she saw a large bird, a raptor, winging in from the east. Hawk, eagle, or osprey? She couldn't tell; it was too far off. She reached for binoculars, which this day did not hang from her neck, a concession to her mother for the special occasion. She willed the bird to continue its course, heading toward the chateau. She willed her eyes to see their best and knew then it was a hawk, a Red-tailed Hawk. Could it be? Since returning from Arkansas, she had not seen Ku-Khain.

Heart yearning, Claire saw with acute vision a crimson cross marking the breast—It was Ku-Khain! Gliding high above the tower, the hawk began to circle upward on a thermal. To follow her rising loops, Claire paced around the tower, face to the sky. Once around, twice around, each time her steps quickening until she felt herself rising upward. Looking over her shoulder, she saw a powerful wing, pumping air. Pulled into a warm wave, she began to circle opposite Ku-Khain, higher and higher inside the tunnel of air, until the tower roof below looked like an orange pebble.

About the Author

Educator turned author, Georgia Anne Butler is writing her third book in the trilogy *Of the Wing,* which follows Claire and her friend Victor through birding adventures in the woodlands of Pennsylvania (book 1), to the bayous of Arkansas (book 2), to the enchanted lakes and hills of Ireland (book 3).

Butler began her career as an instructor of English composition at The Pennsylvania State University. Later she taught in adult education before returning to higher education as an editor and designer of online courses. Under the tutelage of her husband David E. Butler (who died in 2005), Butler became a birder and thereafter conceived a story of a girl with an inexplicable ability to attract birds.

Your Birding Notes

Become a birder starting today! Use these blank pages to keep a list of every bird you see. (The first few have been numbered for you.) You probably already know some birds but most you'll have to learn. Start by finding information on the birds that Claire sees in *Of the Wing*. And follow the author's Bird Blog at

www.ofthewing.com

1.
2.
3.
4.
5.
6.
7.
8.
9.
10.